SLOW CHOCOLATE AUTOPSY

incidents from·the notorious career of **NORTON**, *Prisoner of London*

Iain Sinclair

with illustrations by

Dave McKean

Phoenix House
LONDON

First published in Great Britain in 1997
by Phoenix House.

A CIP catalogue record of this book is available from the British Library.

Typeset by Selwood Systems, Midsomer Norton.

Printed in Great Britain by Butler & Tanner, Frome and London.

Phoenix House

The Orion Publishing Group Ltd.
Orion House
5 Upper St. Martin's Lane
London, WC2H 9EA

SLAM CHOCOLATE AUTOPSY

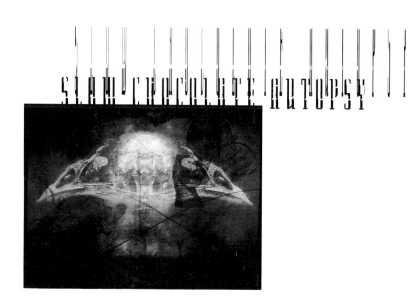

By the same author:

fICTION

White Chappell, Scarlet Tracings
Downriver
Radon Daughters

DOCUMENTary

The Kodak Mantra Diaries (Allen Ginsberg in London)
Lights Out for the Territory

POETry

Back Garden Poems
Muscat's Würm
The Birth Rug
Lud Heat
Suicide Bridge
Flesh Eggs & Scalp Metal: Selected Poetry
Jack Elam's Other Eye
Penguin Modern Poets 10
The Ebbing of the Kraft
Conductors of Chaos *(Editor)*

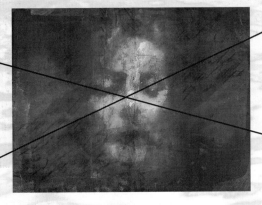

By the same illustrator:

GraPHIC NOVELS/NOVELLas

Violent Cases *(with Neil Gaiman)*
Black Orchid *(with Neil Gaiman)*
Arkham Asylum *(with Grant Morrison)*
Signal to Noise *(with Neil Gaiman)*
Mr. Punch *(with Neil Gaiman)*
Voodoo Lounge *(with The Rolling Stones)*
Cages

MONOGraPHS/PrINT

A Small Book of Black & White Lies
The Tip of my Tongue
Anthropomorphik
The Vertigo Tarot

BOOKS for CHILDrEN

The Day I Swapped My Dad for Two Goldfish *(with Neil Gaiman)*

C O N E N T S

For Alan Moore, Peter Whitehead and the Northampton mystagogues.

NEAR THIS SPOT LIE THE MORTAL REMAINS

CHRISTOPHER MARLOWE

WHO ... UNTIMELY DEATH

... DEPTFORD ...

The *Fifth* Man

Cut is the branch that might have grown full straight

Doctor Faustus

in **i** *the* Garden

with these relics burn thyself
[Christopher Marlowe]

the FiFth mAn in the gARden

*N*orton, no question, was there in the garden when the incident occurred. Early summer, evening. Memories of other evenings, other summers, bringing no tears to his eyes. Hay fever outlived. Enough of the romantic left to enjoy a bench in the shadows, the play of light, the tang of the river – curing sheds, fleshing pits, the vats of the dye makers. Movement re-experienced at rest, travelling shots summarising projected walks. Dark doorways through which Norton glimpses, as he strides, sweating but without purpose or destination, mounds of brilliant colour. Blues, yellows, scarlets. Open yards with glistening alps of sand. Chemical wildernesses. Past fancies, a speculative future. The drench of uncut grass, gloving flowerheads, distant bells, children, pewter plates banged down on oaken tables: all contributed to the illusion of it, the fraudulent sense of place. That this time, this ill-defined moment, was special, singular. Worth fixing. An entry in his black notebook.

He stood by the river wall, anticipating the next breach, the tons of restless, devitalised water. Housing, upstream of the Ravensbourne, was, and knew that it was, transitional. Wattle huts. Thatched fire traps. Tilted sties. The pigs had the best of it, gorging themselves in windfall orchards, drunk enough on earth liquors to relish the prospect of the knife. Why did Norton bother? Why did he flog out, four hours on the loose, up and down the strand, negotiating poisonous industrial premises, panting against the hot walls of warehouses, hoping, against all previous experience, for some solution? More to the point, why did he come back? Bed down on the straw for another night at Ma Bull's crib. How did he find himself in Deptford? He couldn't even spell the word. Debt. Empty pockets. That was the start of it.

Every afternoon, the same mocking glitter of the wavelets. The clock of tides. Norton waited, watched the colour of the water, read it like a horse doctor. Looked for some change, a craft that would risk putting ashore, taking on cargo, moving into a different story. Always the same old ex-crement, bronze to mud. To khaki. Shit Creek, literally. The sink wherein the city's filth is poured. Sediment swirling where it wants to set. Gravelled beaches unmade. Even Norton's funeral coat, black to the ankle, was starting to rust. He had waited for months now on the promise of a Lime-house skipper. That one day a boat without a name would pick him, carry him out of it. Burwell with his crew of fanatics, recusants. Running bales of sea-green hash, resin blocks that had Tyndale bibles hidden inside them. Running unsponsored artists, film crews with no film in their cameras. Mad quests in the coastal reaches. The scuppers awash with sour wine and last night's botched couscous. Tomatoes scarcely out of the tin before they were spewed back on deck. The cook, in his bloody apron, cackling like a Bedlamite.

Burwell had been chartered to make a feint at the off-shore forts, a run at some Spanish powder vessel, gone aground at the mouth of the Medway. He'll take anything aboard that slurps and slops as it's trundled. Uses wineskins for life preservers. You never saw such a rout of dysfunctionals. Any riverside scum up for a jolly. Lunatics waving charts of fever islands, rambling of sunken treasure. Pox skeletons wrapped in quarantine flags. Basket-cases hot to experience their worst nightmares and live to tell the tale. They're crossing themselves, deep into the account of their last drowning, before they stagger up the gangplank. Piss artists, all of them. With their jail-bait, flaky females cozened out of drinking clubs. Totties with virulent nails to grip the wheel. Any excuse to come aboard, work a passage. On their knees if necessary.

Burwell casts off in the dark, no navigation lights showing, nudges his way out on a running tide. Hopes for the best. Twine-handled knife in his teeth, up and down the craft like a monkey with a firework up his jacksy. Raft, rudder, cabin roof. Flailing with a hand-axe, splintering the deck boards to make a decent fire. Hip flask of pink paraffin to coax warmth. Gargles with it before he rounds Cuckold's Point, ignites his own mouth with a gangrenous cigar stump. Dragon-breathed to the galley.

Or so Norton, the weary hack, imagines. So he would like it to be. Another romp. Another disastrous excursion. Fit only for comic book fiction. Direct video release. But Burwell was Norton's best chance. That's why he walked and waited, walked again, fetched up alongside the Dog and Duck steps. Reeling above their untrustworthy verticality. Green bile slopping, higher and higher towards him, as his hopes plunged. Not today. The bung wasted in his pocket. He would peel off another note for Ma Bull, her large hands. Patch of coarse skin at the knuckles, rough as a cat's tongue. Another night marooned in the deadlands. He'll need some business soon. The syrettes of morphine tartrate on offer in Glisters. The Tommy gun. Another night nursing his drink in a trashed nightspot, waiting on rumours. Norton shivered. Ran a sleeve across his damp forehead. Smeared his spectacles with his shirt-tails. The city wouldn't forgive him so easily. For every journey there had to be some innocent to take the bolt, some fall guy. That's what it was all about, earning Charon's wages.

The four men had been fed and watered. Ma Bull was making a production out of clearing the table, opening the garden door, freshening the atmosphere. No chance of Norton trousering a hunk of bread, or a few crumbs of cheese, before the widow sent the girl in. He watched: a gaunt shadow across the leaded window. If there was a bone left, one of these pistols would suck it dry. Nothing foreign about Ma's cuisine: week-old stockpot, bacon on a string, cabbage leaves with an earth basting. Worms a bonus. The four of them, the conspirators, hydra-headed, sweating faces dipped over the tureen. Four crimson masks on one pair of shoulders. Disputing every last prawn husk, tonguing the cold gravy. Ballast for battle-hardened bellies. Red pepper to encourage a thirst. A horn of sack with a gunpowder chaser.

The best, or least worst, of the hoodlums caught Norton's eye. Cocky runt with a weak charcoal chin-line, pencil moustache like a slash in a suet pillow. Arms folded. White hands hanging loose above an imaginary gunbelt. (*Read*: Audie Murphy, back from Hell after killing 240 Germans, in hock to the Mafia. Money laundering cartel pesos in cowboy programmers. A forty-year-old Billy the Kid doing hard time in an Arizona ghost town.) Soft assassin. Eyes like anthracite. Too much for Norton. Backs off, to his bower. He'll sit this one out.

'Poley.' That's what Norton hears. A name or an insult. He's the chancer trying to give some form to this seven-hour riot. One of the others, scalp half-shaven, rings in his nose, calls for more wine. Norton will give it a miss. He can see blood spreading across the table. The spilled claret. The shadow of a dead man left on the wood when they carry him to the mortuary. The four dudes are dicing. They don't know yet. Who will take the blade. Who will slip away into the night.

Their language was too ripe for Norton. Too metaphysical. Too body-based. Heats and humours. Sweats and lascivious pricks. Alchemy. Geography. Astrology. Norton benched himself. Were they connected? From their talk it was clear that they travelled, in and out of the Low Countries as the whim took them. They had names, papers, coins of their own minting. He'd watch and he'd wait.

An enclosure. Trees as a screen. Licensed ground. Where was the gash? The mullet-mouthed crumpet? Breasts jiggling like the W of 'wave'. Mud-splashed skirts raised above glistening buttocks. Gorgeous ginger bushes. When the sugars and foul meats burnt in their guts, when the wine fumes clouded their consciousness, they'd call for cunt. Unless they went the other way. This Poley, with his Tartar eyes, his meat-hook grin, looked like an ambidexter. Then it would get sticky. They'd been drinking all afternoon, taking a turn in the grounds, then back for another jug. It would end in a poking. One way or the other. Ma Bull better padlock her sleeping quarters. Send the girl out for a couple of Winchester geese. Norton wasn't one of those featherbrains who claim to see auras, but even he couldn't miss it this time. Flames rearing from their scalps. Purple tongues. Fire cones to shame the priapic buddleia. Woozy bees. Scents that had him reeling. His face, if they glimpsed it in this mood, would be an invitation to target practice. A white disk hung from an apple tree.

He scuffled his pockets for script. A motto. 'As for myself, I walk abroad a-nights,/And kill sick people groaning under walls.' That's better. When the narrative sticks, pinch a couple of lines from a better man. Write them for him. Leave them lying about where he's sure to find them. Infiltrate the future.

Norton spread the loose pages across his lap. Jaded scribbler. How had he managed to write this stuff without gagging? What did these hophead charts mean? More like a photocopied legal document than a work of literature. What his chum Cookie always called the 'general contract'. Nothing general about it, son. We've all made our mark. In our own stories. Or so it seems. To us. Like Hamlet, Norton thought. He'd landed himself with the revenger's role in a blood and thunder melodrama. And the crime hadn't happened. The corpse had failed its audition. An Italian play with iced arteries. It was like trying to find your way out of somebody else's nightmare.

'I'm a fucking ghost with a bit part in an autobiographical tragedy. Too many lines and nothing to say.' That's the syndrome: being forced to take centre stage in a production that has no appeal. A story that doesn't hold water.

Norton blue-pencilled any speech that went beyond three words. Busied himself for hours. Worked his way through the continuity boxes. Abort all narrative links. Let the picture take the strain. Four men perambulating the circuit of the garden. Two-by-two. Like Dominicans. Low-budget mono-chrome. Poley had his arm around his partner's neck. If only Norton could sketch a true likeness. Images can be reinterpreted at leisure. Words are active. They set up their own force field. Ruffians. Were this quartet the originators of that word? Soiled-collar merchants. Wax heads on paper plates.

The clink of cans. Youths necking it at the graveyard gates. Smoking on sepulchres. Packet-sellers razoring their stock with corpse moss. Giant skulls on gateposts. They don't see Norton. He's of no account, doesn't register. The four men break into three and one. Micturating. The others flank the solitary pisser. Four in a line scorching the hibiscus. The walnut tree. Shadows under shadows. Turf soft as down from a virgin's armpit.

He needs liquidity. He needs a way out, this man. Rumours of surplus weaponry. A drudge on the market. Teenagers webbed into the triads. Machetes at the school gates. Belgian ordnance in a Lewisham bedsit. The old skills redundant. No more shotgun barrels sawn off on kitchen tables. No way to turn an honest penny. Norton outside Glisters, he rattles the door. He knew men who knew men. He had pockets filled with inactive numbers. 'Closed for the duration, mate.' Deptford didn't want to know. He was surplus to requirements. The air, down by the river, was thick with splinters. Broken craft rotting into the foreshore. Elizabethan wood making visible the gentle breeze. Wind you could taste.

Back at the steps. The tide dropping. No Burwell. Nothing out there. Barges of landfill. The pleasure boat Hollywood with its painted promise, to carry fee paying tourists downriver 'To Where Time Begins.'

Norton spat. He cursed the drunks, the riparian scavengers. Burwell and Maliverney Catlin. They'd be tied up now to some rubbish float, hefting old iron. The women working and the men drunk at the rail, shouting obscenities. They'd let the tide go, put in to the jetty of an obscure grogshop. Anywhere they weren't known. Catlin spark out in the stern, two glasses in one hand, sour red with a rum sweetener. And in the other fist, brown shrimps dredged from the sewage beds off Southend pier. Claws caught in his whiskers. Buttons gone. Pissing into the water. Witnessed by totties desperate for abandonment. Anything worse than what they already knew. The cutting edge of a Belfast accent. The voyage out at first light. Tomorrow as a new beginning.

Dusk gave shape to the falcon towers. Things came to life. Or settled into a dangerous immobility. Mud wood. Hunting birds that had escaped their callers. Predators imported to cull alien exoticism. Candy floss pigeons that pecked around Norton's boots. Freaks. Brilliant as cockatoos. A tropical luxuriance for the waterside. Squatters from the roof of the dye factory. Dwarf flamingoes. Ingesters of toxic powder. Hawks peddling the air, the spread of them, claws extended. Killings that Norton did not need to witness.

He ironed out the pages McKean had sent him with the ball of his fist, shuffled the order, but could make no sense of them. 'Unedited city.' There was no way of accessing this data.

'How, friend, is this to be understood? A griffin's egg? Mere devilry and juggling.'

The moustache had crept up on Norton. A Cambridge pedant with a sneer in every sound he committed. The dude was bored with his companions, who were trying, hopelessly, to make a sixpenny dagger stick in the flesh of the walnut tree. 'In all the science I have conned, griffins lay no eggs.'

'Take a hike, shirtlifter.'

'Dialogue not your thing then?' returned the smartarse. 'Unschooled in dispute. Leave cross-talk to the pros, my son.'

It looked interesting for a moment. Norton felt for his shiv. He'd carve the punk. And those black eyes were up for it: choreographed violence. The Cantab smirked. Moved nicely. Faster than he appeared. Language a smokescreen. A psycho in black velvet, optioning mischief. But then his associates, not wanting the affair to climax prematurely, pulled him away. He gestured obscenely with a single digit, piped a song. Clear as a castrato, as they bundled him towards the house.

> 'But see, Achates wills him put to sea,
> And all the sailors merry-make for joy;
> But he, rememb'ring me, shrinks back again.
> See where he comes. Welcome, welcome, my love!'

Norton, furious, whittled a broken branch to a sharp point. He knew now what was coming, the end of it. The trick would be how to put a spin on such an obvious narrative device, how to keep the yarn out of the hands of the conspiracy freaks. How to muzzle Anthony Burgess. God forbid that Ackroyd should pastiche this one. Death, what a banality! And no cast to work with. Four hoods and one outsider. Norton didn't belong. He messed up the symmetry. Norton was going to take the hit. Narrator as victim. That old trope.

The branch was hot in his hand. He'd like to reconnect it to the tree. To pull out of this one, the treason that he hears across the drugged garden. The blasphemy: the Angel Gabriel as bawd to the Holy Ghost. Mary impregnated by her favourite son. The talk of Zion. Of plots and counter-terrors. Norton doesn't want to hear, but the branch has become a kind of wand, an aerial. Removed from the action, he is pressed tight against their lips. His friend, the Cambridge poet, directs the others: Poley, Skeres, Frizer. A play in a shaded corner, a grove. The trees form a theatre, open to the stars. Star blossom. Spiders' lace. Bird-spit. The distant figures are hierophants. The play is a slow ritual. Pin men. Puppets. Every whisper loud in Norton's ear. Surveillance acoustics for the spook, the time-surfer. He sees the threads from their shoulders that leave them swinging from the broad branches. Villainy brought to book. Crow meat. He sees the wind take them. The empty sockets. Skin the colour of dead honey. Norton doesn't want to know. He despises theatre, as it is enacted. As it fails, precisely, to reduplicate itself. At the whim of actors. He likes it in his head, the dream. The sleep tape. A past that's still to come. Where death is a demonstration. And sex-milk gushes in the form of a golden falcon.

Now Norton is bored with the show. His own interpretation. It's too obvious, how they set the poet up, push him to damn himself, flatter his fancies. They'll bring him down by nodding at his speeches, applauding his conceits. If you want to destroy a poet, first publish him. Allow him readings, performances. Let him dance to judgement. They do all that, but it's not enough. He hasn't made his curtain call. Such clownish names as Skeres and Frizer will never skewer a principal. They're a knockabout turn. Hitmen with personal hygiene problems. 'Sir, I will.' That's the only line they're ever going to get.

This Marlowe is a future dick: Dick Powell. He's got Chandler on his case. Humphrey Bogart and Robert Mitchum in his veins. Whisky cancer coating his tongue. A lethal injection creeping inexorably towards the heart. His cloak decays into a mildewed trenchcoat. *The Big Sleep* is the screenplay he never completed. Nobody else could unravel the complexities of the plot. He's got so much future to use up. If one of these punks reaches for a dagger, he'll blow him away.

Deptford needs this comedy. It's a featureless satellite. They still call it West Greenwich. A dull stretch of riverfront must ground itself with a notable crime, something to pad out the History Trail brochure. Marlowe, sleuthing, has already checked St Nick's. Noted the skulls on the gateposts, the blunt church tower.

He has photographed the blank tablet set into the boundary wall. Seen it as a challenge, an empty continuity box in an unfinished graphic novel. *Near This Spot Lie The Mortal Remains Of* . . .

It's unresolvable. Norton wants to be out on the river. Wants to be free of London, all the trash of history. Voices, whispers, busking ghosts, comic strip chimeras. Real fictions and fabulous projections with authentic birth-certificates. Burwell's boat exists. It was there once in Limehouse basin. It was fixed to a buoy, off The Prospect of Whitby. But it's also an illusion. A nightmare. Going down with all hands, the Isle of Sheppey on the starboard beam. Radio relaying afternoon theatre. Pirate spectres on offshore forts. Deserted falcon towers. Drug runs.

There is no Norton. He's a paragraph in a pulp novel. Fifty-thousand copies in drug stores across the United States of America. Yellow dust. An invented name gifted him by a junkie. An invented name to rechristen a dead man. Dead now. Forgotten in his meat identity. Alive in crude print. Name rubbed from the paper. A coffee-stain in a Times Square hash joint.

The carved stick is no wand to be broken, it's a crutch. Norton promises to fling it in the water, if Burwell can carry him successfully through the Thames barrier. If he can get away. Be released from this endless tale-telling.

Marlowe slips his stooges. Frizer and Skeres, as he instructed them, had their arms linked behind his back. Rocking him. Backwards and forwards towards a candle that had been set on a table, brought out into the garden. Poley stood off, unsure of his role. A thatch of low branches crowning his head with horns. Was he required in this scene? Or was he an understudy, an unreliable witness?

Closer and closer to the candle's flame. Eyes wide enough to accept a miniature of the scene. A small tragedy etched on a convex lens. Norton, in his bower, can smell the scorched hair. Can't help himself. Sees the film play itself out in frozen longshot. Sees the way it cuts. He knows the instructions he will have to write, so that McKean will be able to make a sequence of drawings. Work on a convincing reproduction. Classics Illustrated. Some novel like *The Master of Ballantrae* laid out in the style of the Egyptian Book of the Dead. Colour. Corpse revival. Robert Louis Stevenson, legless in Edinburgh, notices the poster peeling from a black granite wall. Sees the flick-book that inspires him, curses him. Fever sleep. The story that must be told as an act of restitution.

Marlowe, poet and espion, has their attention. Their eyes on the candle flame. The spill of shadows making a single hydrocephalic head. Norton breaking time into a stutter of single frames. Close-ups, wide shots. Marlowe, unexpectedly, rushing straight at the camera. As Norton lifts his hands to protect himself. Lifts the sharpened branch. In time to pierce the hot eye, spear the brain jelly. It grinds, it snaps in the wound. A root in the socket of bone.

'It felt,' Norton subsequently wrote, 'as if my finger had become trapped in his head.' The essay was not a success and he destroyed it. But the intemperate ideas that formed the background to the essay, the rush that came to him as he walked through Deptford back towards Tower Bridge, dodging development scams and Holiday Inns, still worried him. Norton floated a curious thesis: that the death of Christopher Marlowe in the garden of the Widow Bull, after a day of conversation and drunkenness, was self-willed, suicide, a triumphal flourish in keeping with his reputation as a playmaker. Cut is the branch. And burned the bough that sometimes grew within this learned man. Now the marble finds its inscription. Now Marlowe's immortality is secure.

Norton has lost his chance of escape. Marlowe is assured of his place in the pantheon, the book of conspiracy. He has reserved his yard of earth. A smart operator, a marvellous boy gone in the teeth. Beating Kyd. Getting out of the game without the help of Maliverney Catlin. Without the caress of the rack. A candle for a bonfire.

The witness pays the reckoning: Norton. The last of his readies. Quits the river. Back inland, drudging the foothills. Heading west. Palaces and

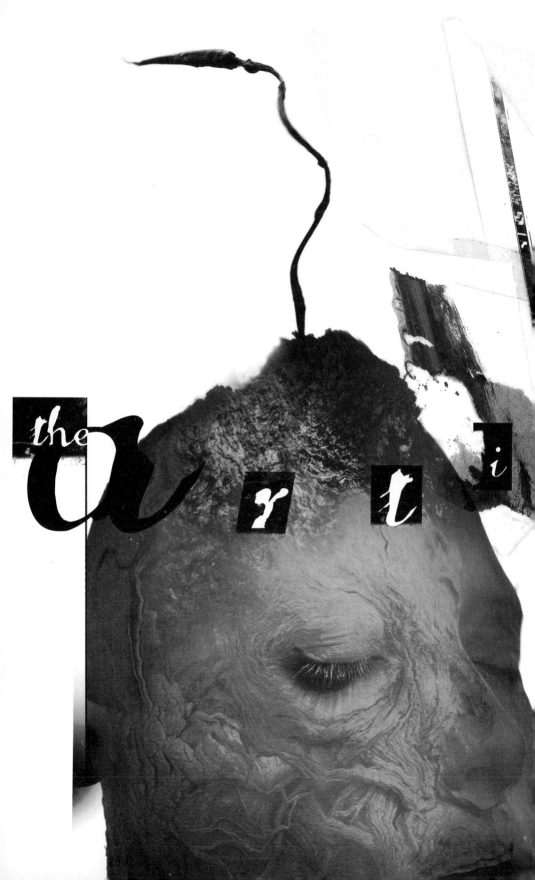

culate ii

head

I will never really leave here now
B. Catling as Cyclops

the ARticulAte heAd

I will never really leave here now
B. Catling as Cyclops

*T*elling him about what happened was the price I paid for the job at the factory. For the old man's tip. For getting me over there ahead of the mob. Somehow he knew about it even before the notice was pinned to the door: *Short Term Labourer Required*. I would have to hold on to the events of the day, rehearse them in my mind, edit them if you like, as I walked back across the waste ground. Make a mental note of everything I saw, sketch the jodhpurred girl as she struggled to bolt the horse stall. Closing away everything except the stink. The hot animal smell that overrode, as you passed the entrance to the yard, the acidic wood pulp of the veneer shed, the sourness of the man-made lake. I'd watch the fountains, the women airing their bundles, and

I'd know, again, the hopelessness of this place. The horizontal despair on which I fed and thrived.

He didn't need to ask. To invoice the debt. His door, at the turn of the stairs, had been left open. He could hear my key in the lock, the struggle to make it bite. My hesitant footfall as I tried to adjust to the profound darkness of the boarding house. My boots tapping against the overhang of the creaking steps. He was always waiting. It didn't matter what time I came in. Two mugs, steaming, ready brewed on the oilcloth. Orange tea with an oily slick on the surface, as if the cheap electroplating had come away from the teaspoon. Tea that was never comfortable to drink, scalding the soft palate – and then, when you missed the optimum moment, as you always did, cold as water from a frozen ditch. Two wedges of bread and cheese on a tin plate. A lick of lard from the bottom of a cat's tray: welcome as a visible penance. A communion of shame. Eating, I was excused speech. He sat on the bed. I stood, my back to him, staring out of the window. Struggling for words that might give form to the meaningless impressions I retrieved from the outside world. Fantasies, observations. The small happenings that remind us of other happenings, paragraphs in abandoned newspapers, things we overhear. I would have preferred to read him an extract from a shabby book or a magazine. But he had none of these in his room. I pictured a house built on piles of moldering pornography, a reservoir of the stuff, but all I ever found, searching the unoccupied basement and the coal-hole, was a suitcase of vegetarian tracts.

'Bullion's on the stove,' he said. He behaved like a blind man, although, as far as I could judge, he wasn't. He swivelled his head to trace the source of any sound, but his eyes were dead as milk. Sometimes he hid them behind the dark glasses he squeezed beneath his habitual balaclava. 'Spoon's in the drawer.'

That was one of his peculiarities. Discovering – a small fiction I had embroidered to keep him amused – that I'd done a couple of terms in college, he began to translate the menu into French. He liked to try his hand at onion soup, metal-green skins floating in a pan of tepid water. It took me a while to work it out. 'Bullion' was his way of pronouncing bouillon. Which, in any case, had nothing to do with onions. He was a furious autodidact, and probably dyslexic (before the term was invented).

But there wasn't much you could slip past him. He could play back any day's journey that you'd undertaken, borough to borough, market to market, by the smell of the muck on your boots.

'Found a salt yet?' he'd ask, the meal over, the bottle of stout drained. 'Something to keep you warm in winter?' Then he would – you could see them through a slash in the black wool – bite his lips. Make noises. Swallow spit.

A woman is what he meant, gash. As I learnt from skimming a book about skinheads that I found on the factory floor. A bit of a book, actually, ten or twelve pages. 'Sorts' is what they call peer group females. Sorts or salts, it's the same thing. Culinary or predatory, no need to be told. I always finished up thinking of Lot's wife, desert jackals licking at her ankles with blue tongues.

Give him his due, the old cunt, he'd never miss when there was work going. He'd give you the word. Hospital kitchens, draying a stall of fruit and veg, scraping chocolate from a flooded toilet stall with a toothbrush: not on for it himself, he'd have you first in line. Up to the gonads in a septic tank, you could thank him for it. How did he make the connection? Never, so far as I knew, went out. Never left the Island.

When I'd had the cheese in my mouth long enough to soften it, I rinsed with cold onion water and spat the rest back into the pan. Turned to the window, the lake, bowls of weak light all along the edge of the rippling water. A distant surf-roar of traffic, unseen, somewhere beyond the park's perimeter. On a good night, there'd be a few stars – flaws in the glass, scratches on the cornea. Blink and you'd miss them. Dogs howling for the loss of the canal. Kids calling each other over, wanting some explanation for a headless rat that had crawled a couple of inches out of the clag.

He'd been here all his life, so he said. Golden days, all that old bollocks, tenements as far as the eye could see. Uncles fiddling the docket down in Southwark, under the arches. Trips on buses. The ruins and the bomb shelters. The prefabs that outlived their weak-lunged occupants. Piss-ups and punch-ups. Psychopaths carving out scrapyard reputations. A suicide, seen through a window, who'd been dead so long he had the best tan in Camberwell. Purple chocolate, he was. A premature time-sharer.

Let him ramble, dredge. What did it matter if he wanted to resurrect that proletarian fable, the rank canal? That's what he missed most, coming back, a visible border. A line beyond which no member of the tribe could safely travel. He'd been away for years, warmer climes, maybe that explained the greatcoat, gloves, balaclava. Now he was back for good, back on the Island.

The canal meant nothing to me, its loss didn't disturb my mental map. I'm a country boy. Prick me, scrape the skin, and I ooze rivers of rust, fern cancers. I dream hillsides and conifer plantations. I drift through ancient graveyards, worrying at erased inscriptions. I caper under a white sheet, a horse's head in place of my own. I jangle like a tinker. False memories. If I could find the pen I once had, who knows, I might make something of them. Like fuck I would.

In truth, he didn't have much to say about this canal, which was now filled in, covered with concrete, but it was an important symbol. Speech didn't come easily to him. To either of us. His teeth were a broken fence. Paleolithic. They dated him. They belonged in the mouth of an extinct crocodile. Living fossils. You wouldn't be surprised to find the outline of one of them pressed into a stone in the mud of his precious canal. From that single tusk, you could invent the rest. Enough was too much, more than I could bear to hear.

His mouth, as the room declined into darkness, moved on its own. Those electrical teeth chattering compulsively in a birth camp. Teeth that were older than he was. Liar's teeth that could persuade you to do anything, kill or cure, suborn or adulterate, deny whatever you loved best. Now he was brokering the canal as a clamped section of vein, a tied-off junkie's arm. I turned away from him. I couldn't watch. I let his words inform the dim landscape. This was, by love, his estate. By informed hatred. Intelligence. His vision charmed the dog-scorched hummocks. The intimacy he displayed, that grudging, phlegmy growl, had a tenderness that was essentially sexual. He curated the turf, the yellow gravel. His finger teased the lake's hymeneal surface. Droplets of water, as he flicked them, became bird-light. He possessed everything that he did not desire. Listening to him, sharing his exile, I became his surrogate. I walked out of there in his place.

'Get yourself down the factory,' he said, one morning, when he heard me coming back from the baker with a bag of throwout bagels. 'Alongside where the art school used to be, Peckham Road.'

And he was right. They did want someone, a person capable of demolishing a freestanding interior wall, pink as Caladryl lotion. Take it down, bag it, chuck it in a skip. No problem, except for one thing. The Factory stood just beyond home territory. Fifty yards or so, enough to make me uneasy. I liked to stay within the limits of ground shaped like a goat's head: Albion Road as the crown of the skull, Southampton Way and Trafalgar Avenue as the cheekbones. The Island in the middle of it, in the waste of abandoned parkland and pre-development tundra. The Island in an island. Why take any chances? Why provoke fate? Such a depth of obscurity was hard-earned, but cashmoney was cashmoney.

I worried too much, peed too often into the silted basin. It was a good number, one of the best. Left alone to do the business in my own time. Cash in hand. Stretch it out, if I didn't go mad, over three or four days. The blokes who took me on knew nothing about graft. Suits and spectacles, they were; hardhats clamped down over their tight curls before they would so much as talk about the job. No intention of scuffing their black brogues inside the building.

It had been a long time, years, since I'd had a pick in my hands. I was never too bright at remembering the names of the instruments, the work tools. I was brute force, what Stevenson called a 'handless' man. I worked because it was all I could get. I liked it better than sitting in halls of strip-lighting, filling in forms, catching up with all the latest viruses. I preferred to stay out of the files, the books of reference. When I died, that would be it, no trace, nothing to keep me here. You'd never find the directory from which I'd been excluded.

They left me with plenty of gear. A spade you could call a spade. A heavy duty hammer and a sharpened steel bar, bigger and more dangerous looking than a cold chisel. Serious intent in this kit. Do some proper damage in the wrong hands. The tools invented their own crimes. They yarned like mouthy gangsters, like Saturday night in the Becket. Plenty of black bags supplied for the rubble. They split, so I discovered, as soon as you used them. I tied my insides in knots wrestling the slippery sacks across the wood floor, up the steps, through the entrance hall, down some more steps, and out into the road. A bunch of jeering marble heads on a shelf made me want to take a harpoon to their patronising neutrality. Dead white flesh. Eyes blind to the tribulations of labour.

But, taken all in all, this was as good as it gets. Make sure you have a broom in the hand come six o'clock and you've nothing to worry about. The Nigerians wanted the wall out, gone, the rest was up to me. I was my own site manager. I expect there was paperwork somewhere, requisition orders in triplicate, an approved budget. Not my affair. The guvnors had to have something in their silver cases, apart from the mobiles, the A–Z and the designer shades. That tailoring was a piss-take. They talked to each other, never directly to me. I was supposed to eavesdrop, read their lips. I might as well have been invisible. Which was very perceptive of them. It's why they had the BMW and I had the callouses. They were risk takers. I was a coward, indulging the old acid. Sneering at those who had the bottle to make themselves repulsive. The ones who lived and prospered in the here and now.

Leave aside the dust, the cobwebs, the stringy turds screwed up in spills of newspaper, and the place was not in bad nick. It had been closed down for a long time. Doors shut, forgotten about. Beyond sponsorship. I sat on the steps for most of that first morning, indulging an unexpected rush of calm. Nature's Librium: carbon monoxide, lime trees, rubber boots. The purposes to which the room had once been put flooded back on me. Believe them or believe them not. The dead voices of teachers making public pronouncements, or whispering encouragement, jokes and asides, as they walked around the hunched students, inspecting their work. Young women in smocks had sat on uncomfortable chairs, boards in their laps, copying the curve of a naked model's spine. I saw a man on a sort of podium. Thin, hollow chest, ribs like a swallowed toast-rack. Red hair. Two growths on his scalp, flesh strawberries. One of the women concentrated on this spectacular deformity, this baroque decoration. Given a choice, she preferred working with corpses, claw hands, gas-filled bellies, peeled skulls. But these were rarely available. She treated the man's head like a still life. She saw, within the throbbing bulb of veins, its shining surface, the homunculus. The flawless other. The teacher commended her skill, her vision. The ability to transmute, to begin with precisely observed particulars and to open them out into a narrative so grand that it was, in all but name, operatic. Dissecting those purple-red growths produced a sound, a score. I could hear it. Hear what the older man, stumbling awkwardly in his language, his commitment to praise, said to her.

The naked figure – stooped over, dozing, elsewhere, as I was, as I identified with him – became a patient. An out-patient. A smudged face in a pre-war photograph, waiting in a hall as large as this one, waiting for attention, a verdict. It was *this* hall. A clinic for weak chests, industrial accidents, consumption, diseases still to be named. The hall had bustled with postal workers, grey sacks, death letters, official commiserations, adulteries brutally revealed. A loved one's sputum licked from the cruel V of the envelope's flap.

The model, exposing his genitals, but covering his deformity with a vast white hand, snored, but held his pose – unsure if he would wake to a session of chemotherapy or an act of love. A tiled cell or an unfamiliar doss house. He needed to work a splinter from the bench into the meat of a hangnail to reassure himself that his floating perceptions were not entirely posthumous.

The wall I was supposed to knock down had no obvious purpose. I didn't try to invent one. Given a morning in its presence, sizing it up, I began to imagine shapes on its surface. The light was untrustworthy. The high roof with its tilted glass panels, so useful to the art students, had been largely blacked out. Dim shafts fell, at the end of the room, on the far side of the wall. That is where I went first, tapping down the right side – and then exploring, to see what was there, at the back of the obstacle. The answer was nothing. Daylight. A puddle of revealed floorboards.

I tried again. Walked up to the wall, confronted it. Neither of us would give an inch. But I was the one holding the sledgehammer. (The name came to me as I swung. Nothing like any sledge I'd ever seen.) Plaster puffed around the point of impact. No grievous hurt. Let that be a warning, I thought.

I hated this powdery, analgesic pinkness. I laid out the black rubbish bags in a formal arrangement, then went back to the steps. There was only one way of behaving in this room: stick to the true walls, keep away from that fraud with its unrevealed agenda.

I did a bit of sweeping, always therapeutic. I cleared all the irrelevant mess, the papers, bottles, overblown announcements of preposterous art events, non-happenings, choreographed surprises. Tolerated exhibition-ism. The bourgeoisie shocked in its absence, gobsmacked by the failure of imagination. Impossible to tell, now, what was authentic rubbish, and what had been wrenched out of context, bought here in the reckless spirit of surrealism.

Asbestos flakes twirled and twisted, showed themselves off. Pink plaster in horribly dry heaps, like something squitted out by a hairless poodle with an angora habit. Titbits of ex-flesh metamorphosing into clay. Infantile rust. Fibreless tissue. Gummy slag. When I'd gathered up enough of the more solid fragments, the bits with angles and corners, I assembled something that looked like a carriage clock. The kind that is inherited. Unwound on the mantelpiece. Key misplaced. Forty years by some poor sod in the same job and nobody left who even knows his name. The account clerk's tribute. As tragic as castiron curlicues around the door frames and window ledges of Bethnal Green terraces in sepia photographs.

When I heard chimes, I swear it, coming out of the pink wall, I had to clear my head. A splash of water. Back to the Island, keeping that detail to myself.

Next morning I made a proper survey: walked the room, down the right side, back up the left, just as I had done before. There was no other way of handling it. A pause at the rear of the wall, a glance at the uncovered skylight. A nod on the way through the vestibule at the heads of the Victorian worthies, those brassbound moralists with their vision of a society that was still within hailing distance of salvation. Some student had chipped off the tip of G. F. Watts' nose as a souvenir.

Nothing. Nothing there. You have to understand that. Nothing to report. I'd have to take the long way home to think of an image or incident to lay out for the old man. The back of the wall was white, as you'd expect in a gallery, but it was the other side, the pink, that infuriated me. It was too domestic. It had an uncoded language stream within its flaws. Deep shallows, that's how I was forced to read the rectangular surface, the plastered brick screen. The pink wash was keeping speech down, provoking it. At the same time.

As I stood there, at an oblique angle, waiting for the light to grow stronger, reveal more, a shocking thing happened. I heard those chimes again. There was no mistaking them. They were a mocking reference to normality, a normality quotation. My response to this hallucination was completely irrational. I took a hammer to the remains of the plaster clock and smashed them into powder. I swept the powder into a sack and stamped on it, kept stamping until the sack burst. Put that sack into another.

Madness. The chimes could have come from anywhere within the building. What did I know? There might have been others, other labourers, unemployables, dysfunks, carrying out their specified tasks in other rooms, just like this one. Other memory banks were being tapped. Other minds drained, drawn down into the same subterranean tank. Stand still and you could smell them. Tin drums of hair that had been set on fire. The strange coloured urine of tranquillised mumblers who pissed in desk drawers. Spiders caught in porcelain bathtubs of torched washhouses and swallowed at a gulp. There were other men, I was sure of it, building walls of the exact dimensions of the one I had been paid to destroy.

But then, much worse than the chimes, came the voice. A man's voice, feigning drunk to excuse his presumption. Call it, as shorthand, singing. But it was more terrible than that. Distinguish it, by its pitch, its tricks of breath, from plain speech. This was the soundtrack of your worst nightmare. You'd slipped into the most obscure pub on the Island, bought your pint of stout, hidden yourself in a corner, when it began. You couldn't abandon your liquid investment. You couldn't draw attention to yourself by doing a runner. You're stuck there for the duration. A quiet drink on a weekday night, that was the height of your ambition. And a drunken clown, swaying on varnished hooves, loosening a yellow silk tie, Brylcreem snails oozing down his neck, chucks *Some Enchanted Evening* in your face. 'All right, ladies? All right, Dawn?' A plastered crooner, sofa-hair bursting through his shirt buttons, fiddling with his boxer shorts for the most comfortable hang, hits you with Rossano Brazzi. A six pint gigolo. 'Arright, guls?' Rodgers and Hammerstein. A loop of horror that has the pink plaster sweating, that conjures the lineaments of a face out of the rough surface. Sentiment like a slap of cold cod.

I rushed around to the other side of the wall. And the sound died. Died with the brightening day. I waited, squatting on the floor, until my knees locked. Crawled back. Light equalled silence.

I had to stare this thing out. The crude brush strokes that had applied the pink wash to the wall took, if you insisted upon it, the outline of a man's head and shoulders. It was there and it wasn't there. It played with you, solicited darkness. Turn and it appeared to move. Stains, discoloured patches that favoured the original pattern of the bricks, offered a bulbous and shifting mugshot. A bloater, a dogfish transfer. A translucent jelly that took in water and gave out blood. The wall was a tank of tainted amniotic fluid. I pulled out my tin and fished for a peppermint. I sucked hard, trying to coax some spit into my dry mouth. I had the idea that the ring of mint would act like garlic on the apparition.

Take what I saw, or thought I saw, as the relic of a failed fresco dauber, a confession. Some feeble icon-shaping instinct was alive in me. The pink wall contained a Turin shroud heat print, a genuine forgery. Whatever ceremony had been enacted in that room was there still. The afterburn of an obscene invocation. As the light faded, it got worse – the room lost its form and the head on the screen became more sure of itself, better defined. With the door behind me open, and beams of passing traffic sweeping across the wall, I began to feel that I was the subject of this gross portrait. All my secret shames were fed into the masonry. The amorphous head was an illegitimate brain scan, an unrequested X-ray.

The voice was coming out of a savage, and otherwise undocumented, past. Its even tones held to an insistent present tense. Its utterances were rhetorical, grandiose – but I had to believe them. The head was borrowed from a god hoarding, a Kingdom Hall poster. It represented a salesman in a stiff aureole of hair gel. A coarse denim shirt. A prisoner, a lifer. Self-condemned to the eternity of this abandoned chamber.

I grab the sledgehammer and smash it against the wall, the mouth, that articulate fault. Plaster flakes and crumbles. Brick chips fly like shrapnel. No major damage. I don't have the knack of it, effortless destruction. But I hear the scream, the offensive laugh. Like an old man coughing up boot leather. A gummy foot-fetishist being forced to relinquish a wafer of nylon. He's choking, gagging on ripeness.

I can hear a horn vibrating in the head of this man. The head which is only the ghost of a head. Indestructible. The head which exists as the excuse for a voice. That lives without it. In the plaster. In the dry pink skin. The brick. An unforgiving exploitation of place. A draining of essence. Each breath is a sucking sound. A criminal thirst drinking roses from the flapping wallpaper of memory bedrooms. Refusing to let go. Tooth glass cupped to partition. Eye to keyhole. The peeper in the dark garden. The cur licking its wounds under oilcloth. A suicide's eye view from the attic window of the last tenement on the Island.

These are spellbinding confessions. I listen in wonder, let the sledge-hammer rest. If I stayed here for ever I would never have half as much to say. The longer I remain in one place, the more silent I become. Such elegant traceries of invective, such pitiless scorn. How the head deludes itself, shape-shifts to parade its spectacular deformity. 'I am the monster, the cyclops. Love me for what I know.' It plays with form – a pig's bladder, a floater, a suet pillow. It feeds on its own fat.

I'm looking at the plaster face from the bottom of a well. From beneath the browny pink soup of the canal. From concrete. I'm staring down at a bent moon. The wool in the bottom of a milk bottle. I'm wall-eyed, rubber-legged. Fucked out with the effort of maintaining a contact that I do not desire. Holding the illusion. Focusing it, so that I have a clear target for my hammer. It can't be done. The voice has nothing to do with my perception of it. The voice is embedded in the building.

I step forward, swing and smash. Swing again. A shudder in my wrists. Plaster in an asbestos cloud. Like shaking up a snow scene in a plastic globe. A view of Tower Bridge. The cloud reforms, unchanged. A few bruises under the eyes. A cold chisel lobotomy reinforcing ignorance.

As darkness settles and thickens, quilts the long room, the face reasserts its dominance. The mouth is an eye. The eye a single wooden tooth. A face in the palm of your hand. The head spreads like egg broken in a pan. Like a portrait of the French writer, Flaubert, inflated until it loses definition. Confession disguises crime, takes the heat away from genuine and undisclosed acts of evil. Secrets that do not belong to this territory. These lists of wrongdoings are boasts.

Hypnotic. The mesmerising cadences of that voice, the copper's friend.

The man, the one who has polluted the wall, has done something so bad that it can never be talked about. Easy then to tap the broken turf, mythologise a fictive childhood, celebrate ruin and all the discriminations of loss. That's his difficulty, he doesn't know what he has done. Or if it is yet to come, this unforgivable apostasy. The head is older than the last puddle of water drained from the canal. The last ammonite in the pillar of the brick-windowed chapel.

So, he performs. Yes. Shoulder-shuffles. A nod and a wink. Sump-oil carapace. Bull's spine and string of whelk. Piss and vinegar. Boots resting on the best settee. Karaoke shaman. Brass fly-buttons left as a tip in the saucer.

I batter the wall to a heap. I wreck myself in the act of it. I leave it for another day. A dust mound in an empty room.

This is one night I want to get up to my room without interruption, without the visit, the onion soup, the cheese rind. I want the old man's door to be shut, his hutch in darkness. I want to hear his constricted breathing as I pause on the stair. I'm implicated now, I know too much. I'm frightened that if I open my mouth, a terrible Mockney growl will spew out, the knock-about routines of a concert party Lear. I'll be cutting performance art with gangland justifications. I'll swamp the Island with hairy-knuckled senti-mentality. I'll tapdance on the old man's chest. I'll spike his eyes with my spurs. I'll have an arm around his shoulders, before I crush his ribs like Twiglets. I'll speak in song. I'll soliloquise like a dogtrack spieler. I'll cal-culate in fruit-machine numbers.

Not tonight, let him be asleep. I couldn't bear it, the inch of condensed milk tongued over burnt toast. Waiting for it to spread. The trembling hands hanging on to the gouged tin. The dim eyes behind dark glasses. Let him be dead on his bed. Suffering cardiac arrest in the backyard khazi, the dung hole. Let him venture out and be drowned in the lake by pre-school razor gangs. Let his blue-veined whiteness be torn apart by dog packs, pecked to ribbons by grease-black crows. Fill his mouth with limestone pebbles. Stop him.

A dozen creaking steps in the dark to enjoy this rhetoric. Passive revenger, I know that the door will be open, candlelight flickering within. Unconvinced shadows. Light you have to imagine – like gas jets starting up in a crematorium. Deleted thoughts. First thought best thought, best forgotten.

He had his back to me. Unusually, he didn't look up as I stood in the doorway. Who am I fooling? The day cannot be wiped until I unspool it for him, let him take the burden. But still I dreaded the act of forming a narrative. Why not move on then? Go straight up the stairs. I'll go, get away with it. Into bed. Under the blanket.

He's slumped. Sunk. Collapsed into himself. Head in his hands. It almost appeared, this was my fantasy, that, for the first time since I had known him, he had pulled off the balaclava. The thing was so much a part of him, of the way I described him to myself, the way I recognised who he was, separated him from all the other old men, that I thought, for a moment, he was a stranger. But the posture, the thing they call 'body language', was unmistakable. It was him all right, nobody like him. I'd guessed once that the balaclava was occulting badly burnt skin or a wet graft that hadn't taken. That he was a terrorist in hiding. That he'd absorbed the shock of an urban explosion, the destruction of an office block or medieval church. That he'd failed in his mission and was on the run. He was a maimed victim who chose to wear the uniform of his persecutors. The city was full of such cases. Drinkers. Friends of fire. Bagmen with stiff coats between their bones and the pavement.

His black wool cowl was on the bed. On the grey pillow. The residue of a long-forgotten adulterous event. His rent book was under it, a couple of banknotes folded between the pages. I saw a name, probably not his own. I tried, too late, to avoid it. Norton. It meant nothing. I'm improvising, speaking out of turn. Making outrageous assumptions.

Leave him to it. It's not something he wants to share. I'll sweep up the plaster tomorrow, get rid of the wall. A row of black bags in the skip and it's done. Pouch my money. Think about another job. Think about moving on. Seeing if any other district is as bad. The idea of change, in small increments, is a legitimate pleasure. I'll make a masochist of myself yet, no matter how much it hurts.

He turned, of course he did. No other way out of this. He broke from his reverie. Or, in that movement, made it *all* reverie: the lake, the Island, the tenement. The dream of what is here. Mundane and glamorous. The unnoticed, noticed. The unremarkable, remarked.

There was nothing on the stove, although the hot plate glowed like a burning eye. No food on the table. He twisted towards the sound of me, the breathing I tried to suppress, the violent hammering of my heart. He looked directly into my face. I say 'looked', but that's not quite true. That's not, I must make clear, the full picture.

He was not capable of looking. He had no face. His head, from the neck up, was a kind of thumb. A bolster washed in pink. Runnels of pink had spilled down his vest, over the unbuttoned pyjama jacket. I thought he had a bag over his head, a bizarre act of auto-eroticism. He was groaning, fighting for breath. The focus, as I stared at him, kept shifting. He'd put himself into reverse, to repair the slow confession in the plaster of the wall. To take it back. Now it didn't matter to him. He could turn towards the window. He could absorb that drowned landscape with perfect indifference.

I stepped inside. I pushed past him, picked up the black wool hood and carried it away with me to my room. He said nothing. I put the hood in an empty drawer and then I lay down on the bed.

certain

measurements

of

B ALL

breath

were

iii

evident
[Alan Moore]

hardball

Certain measurements of breath were evident

Alan Moore

The harder I gunned the engine, the worse the wheels spun. I could hear them coming, thrashing through the reeds, calling to me, my name. I couldn't see a thing. The screen was fogged with my panicking breath. I had no idea how to start the windscreen wipers. I was a walker, not a driver. I'd watched the Pole from the passenger's seat, that's all I had to go on. His eccentricity. The way he swore in Polish, spat out of the window. 'Shit on your Arsenal. Shit on beards, Communist wanking bastards. Curly boys, arse-fuckers.' That's what it sounded like. Then he would cross himself.

I put my heel to the pedal. Useless. There was smoke coming from the wheels. I was more likely to end up in the river than to find the track across the marshes. What did the Pole do when we were caught on black ice? He fetched out a sack of ashes that he kept among all the other rubbish in the back. He spread grit and clinker around the wheels. He kicked at the thick tread. 'Lazy wanking bastards.' And it always worked.

I listened. The fog had closed everything down. I couldn't hear them anymore. I chanced it, opened the door. Crept around to the rear of the van. Night sounds were distorted. A weasel crunching a mouse's skull was amplified into a collision of icebergs. My heart was an animal trying to claw its way out of my chest. Any movement, any sigh in the reeds, was a forest fire.

There were two sacks. I had to make my choice by touch. One was tied at the neck with string. It was lumpy with hard round shapes – footballs? The other was slippery, a bin bag. I tore at it with my nails. Ripped it, as if it were the Pole's cheek. I felt the stuff trickle out into my hands. I tasted it. Ash. I dragged the split sack from the van and heaped what I could around the wheels. All of it, all of the sharp bits, the coal splinters, the powder that was as soft as icing sugar. As dream cocaine.

Now they were calling again. It was the kid's voice, turning my name into a joke. He was caught in the undergrowth, blaspheming and yelping like a bitch, then breaking into song. A maniac. I liked him. I'd probably regret it afterwards if I had to stave in his head.

A spade, I'd definitely need a spade. To hold them off or to dig myself out. I fumbled once more through the junk the Pole kept in his van. What the hell did he want with bundles of umbrellas, women's shoes, paperback books he couldn't read, tyres he'd never fit on to a pram? A pickaxe, a broom, a rake. I got my hand on the spade. Left the doors open, rushed back, while there was still time. One last try. The kid was out there, further off. It sounded like he'd blundered into one of the ponds. He was cursing a blue streak. Out of it for the moment, problems of his own.

I heaved myself back into the driver's seat. Gripped the wheel. Deep breaths. Took the clammy grey air down into my lungs, held it like a draw. The pitch of terror was easing. It was going to be all right. I visualised the wheels biting, the van moving off: no lights, pushing a new track through the reeds. Hurtling recklessly towards the sodium necklace marking the road that skirted the industrial estate. That's why none of the street names had been in my tattered A–Z. They were new, optimistic, part of the redevelopment, the low buildings, the units that would all, one day, be occupied and busy. I saw the future, prosperity. I'd get a real job, a wife. I might even learn to drive.

The Pole, who was waiting quietly in the passenger seat, reached across for the keys; switched the engine off, took the keys from the ignition. He wound down his window, spat. 'Fucking Georgi Greyhead Graham, Communist wanking bastard, thief.' Then he patted my knee.

The Pole had never been one for conversation. I worked with him, on the marshes, for three years and got nothing more than grunted orders – recipes for white lime, the number of goalposts required, ritual anathemas on Arsenal, leftists, homosexuals. We didn't see many Afro-Caribbeans among the dog fanciers and coarse-range golfers who patronised the grasslands on weekdays. Which was just as well. Bouncing along in the trailer, behind his tractor, we got used to the way he would come to an unexpected halt. 'Shvartzer!' The cursing would continue until he'd worked up enough of a thirst to dig the vodka bottle out from the inside pouch of the mildewed greatcoat he wore, winter and summer, over a leather waist-coat and a couple of rancid sweaters. Cap, muffler, fingerless gloves.

We always operated three-handed. There were over two hundred pitches to be marked out, a task that was as eternal as the painting of the Forth Bridge. Get to the finish and then start again. I loved the pure geometry of it. I pictured the patterns as they might be seen from the air. White mandalas decorating the green. I loved the width of the skies. Once we'd begun for the day, there was plenty of space to avoid each other. I would see the Pole on the horizon, sitting in the tractor cab, arms folded. Unless I needed to refill my roller, I kept clear of the man, his aura of unquenchable spite.

The casuals who made up the team never stayed long. Two or three weeks was average. The Pole ignored them. Wouldn't answer if they spoke to him, took out a copy of the *Radio Times* and covered his face with it. He didn't have a radio, or a television set, I knew that much. 'Television whore bastard, no good. Eyes, head.' He gestured with two fingers pressed against his eyeballs. He had found the magazine in the tractor when he inherited the job, after one of the wars. Most of the casuals learnt to respect his whims – before they found themselves trying to paint white lines that had the consistency of bone porridge. Before he rolled a cross-bar out of the trailer on to an unprotected foot. Some of these gypos and vagrants were crazier than he was: snackers on dog turds, skeletal naturists, baby faces who licked pus from freshly-squeezed blackheads while boasting of the hits they'd got away with, sheep rapists, grass bulimics, hairtrigger millennialists. White trash too weird to be housed in prisons or asylums.

The worst we ever had was a skull called Norton. He was involved, so they said, in some deal with the Twins that went sour. He was a dead man, waiting for it. Wouldn't get his hands dirty, didn't know how. Lived in the shithouse, book on his lap – until the Pole shopped him. Amen, baby, and good-night.

Aliens couldn't take the marshes. The first teabreak and they were gone. They'd trot into the bushes to enjoy a crap, the more sensitive of them, and never be seen again.

But the kid was a sticker. As well as a speed freak. You could hear him rabbiting from the other side of Epping Forest. Football mad. Chased the Hammers up and down the length of the country. Which was why, like me, it pissed him off to have to work on Saturdays and Sundays. Opening up the changing rooms, cleaning the filth that the amateurs left behind: mud, plasters, shampoo sachets, embrocation, even condoms floating in the trough. What did they get up to? Had they saved the knotted rubbers as a macho boast? Or did a win excite them so much they shot off in an orgy of mutual congratulation? The Pole wouldn't have anything to do with it. Too many black athletes. Too much backchat. He drank fiercely in his tractor, waiting until we were ready to take down the goalposts.

My grouse was that I couldn't play myself. I was a loner, never part of a team, never in thrall to the whistle. Night football was just my way of coming to an understanding with the magnitude of London, seeing it as an anthology of green scraps, fragmented meadows, wastelots, school yards. I cruised as a serial five-a-sider. I'd go anywhere. Set off at random, hop a bus, or simply walk until I was exhausted in a direction that I'd never before attempted. Scuffed trainers, baggy jeans, ready for it. I was a three-and-in, headers and volleys freelancer. I pocketed change (lost it fre-quently) on park challenges. I'd grown up learning to control a wet tennis ball, shooting at a chalked goal, never losing possession – even to another member of my own team. Elbows out, eyes down, no headers, no percentage play, no long punts into space. A Sunday league kickabout or a pub challenge on proper turf gave me agoraphobia. I could do anything with the ball except pass it.

I scored games against black kids turned off the astroturf in Caledonian Park. We dodged traffic for a Brewery Road shoot-out. I cardiac-arrested a trio of retired Scottish postmen on London Fields, clattered their superior skills. I played as a mercenary for a Kurdish mob in an afterhours playground at the back of Ridley Road Market. I kicked lumps out of middle-class pretenders in Regent's Park. I made up the numbers on Tooting Common. I took a few quid off a heritage film-crew in Charlton Park. Through these contacts, nameless encounters, I mapped the city, the shape of its energy patterns.

When the weather turned, and the speed freak was still with us – Julian Dicks crop, mouthy, sweat-ringed black current shirt – the Pole started to take the tractor, in the lunchbreak, down to a strip of grass between the canal and the Hackney Stadium, the dog track. He'd open his *Radio Times* and leave us to it. But it just so happened he had a sack of footballs in the trailer. He let us find them, and, in boredom, use them. Three and in (except that the kid refused ever to come out) against a roughcast wall. An ugly place. The wall in slabs, razorwire above it, on which flapping kits of plastic, wingless birds, signalled the breeze. Earth mounds from the stadium's renovation backed up to the wall, and, beyond the mounds, rows of seven-lamped light towers. It was obviously a favoured site for the Pole. And you could see why. Even the Alsatians that various sullen members of the underclass exercised along the perimeter made him feel at home.

The kid fancied himself as a goalie. Dog shit didn't deter him. He flung himself about in wild abandon, climbed reeking on to the trailer. Indoors, he'd have been unbearable. If I got five shots in succession past him, I won a slug of vodka. If he saved three on the trot, it was his turn at the bottle. Half-pissed, we returned to our white lines. Mine meandered into crazed calligraphy, oval pitches, no corners. I got slower and slower and finally bunked off to doze under the poplars. The kid did his wiz and, pin-eyed, scorched the grass like an Exocet. Tramlines that ran for half a mile. Pitches divided up like chessboards. You could hear him rabbiting on. He swore, against all evidence, against the yelping of hounds, that Orient played in the Hackney Stadium. He'd been there, seen them. Had a trial, been offered terms. He could have been a five grand a week man, trading wisecracks with Barry Hearn. He could have followed the former manager to Forest. He was like every politician you've ever heard of, like David Frost. They could all have been pros. Orient were bollocks. It was the Hammers or nothing.

At the end of the afternoon, when the Pole picked us up, he surprised me. He gestured that he had something he wanted us to see. He fumbled beneath the leather waistcoat and retrieved a yellow packet. Photographs, murky, taken at night, football stadia. Highbury, Loftus Road, the Den, the Valley, Upton Park – even Craven Cottage seen from across the river, as well as from Bishop's Park. They weren't bad. They looked gaunt and sinister, floodlights fogging. Broken-down people's palaces. Tarted up leisure and entertainment facilities. Symbols of exclusion. The Pole's album was like the proposal for a Channel 4 documentary. He lacked White Hart Lane to hook the desktop fantasists.

Apparently, and this was the biggest shock of all, the kid had been helping him, taking him around. The speed freak wasn't bothered about getting into the game, if it didn't involve the Hammers. He'd happily play one-on-one, against the car park wall, with some local urchin, uphold the honour of Plaistow and Forest Gate. There was always a wager which the Pole supervised. He didn't explain, not then, what the stake would be.

'Who do you support?' I asked.

'Football shit. Arsenal wankers.' Only the grounds interested him, the architecture of enclosure, the baying mob. The dogs, the security cameras. The columns of floodlights. Not for nothing had the partisans of Allende been massacred inside a football stadium. Hadn't the Parisian Jews been rounded up in such a place to wait for transport? The Pole wanted to feed on bad karma, the malign passion of the crowd. He would lurk in the shadows and concentrate all that latent mayhem into his camera. Unwatched football was his metaphor of chaos. He didn't need to see the Christians torn apart by lions. It was much more subtle to listen in the deserted street outside, to interpret every nuance that emanated from the trapped punters. Foiled orgasms of sound. Then pick some ragamuffin nobody would miss to play against his feral gladiator.

I agreed to meet them outside White Hart Lane, at the back of the East Stand. The next evening game, an eight o'clock kick-off, happened to be against Manchester United. Insanity. The way the purity of proletarian Saturday afternoons, one time for all, has been shafted by market forces. The crowd reduced to a rabble of high-profile extras. Extras who pay royally for the privilege of dubbing background noise on to a TV special.

A bleak, damp evening in the post-Christmas lull. I walked there, up the Lea Valley, past the marshes, Springfield Park and the old sewage farm. Nowhere open, nowhere to get a drink to lift the choking poultice of oily air. A Scotch egg and a black coffee from a petrol station was the best I could do. I was in an evil mood by the time I found them, parked up in a dirty blue van.

The Pole was eating cold cabbage from a chipped mug, washing it down with the usual drafts of vodka. The kid was chewing on a pig's foot, wiping the grease into his lank hair. A consumptive Eddie Cochran imitator. The foot was a gesture at grossness. He couldn't hack it. No appetite. Dry lips. Curd at the corners of his mouth. Thirsty for a hit of Cola sugar, a tooth-rotting suck at a sticky can. He dropped the nibbled hoof out of the window. Even the rats refused to take the bait. The mindless vandalism was a provocation aimed at the supposed cultural bias of the Tottenham supporters, a fatty compass tossed derisively in the direction of Stamford Hill. Spurs, as far as he was concerned, were the pits. The acceptable face of football, football for tourists from Hampstead, broadsheet dickheads, flabby essayists hymning Gazza as a cock on legs. Football as a cash cow, a way of laundering sweatshop slush funds, insurance barbecues. Sugar by name, salt by nature. The kid ranted like a decommissioned poet.

The game had been in progress for about half an hour when I found them. Even the technicians hanging about in their caravans seemed to think they'd got it right for once. The crowd were going mad, wave after wave of ecstatic roars, an opera of the masses. Thick vine clusters of electric cable ran from the TV vans, over the wall, into the stadium. The electrification of the unwashed. Not a star in the sky, warm air pushing in from the south, hurting the indignant gloom of the Lea Valley, the trading estates, the night-flashing railway, the dead streets with their boarded-up shops. Football turned Tottenham into Belfast. And the entire country, and probably most of Europe and Asia (bets down), were hooked on this, plugged into this unlikely confrontation. Tottenham were stuffing United. Chris Armstrong, the former Crystal Palace charger, the recreational puffer, had glanced in a header that was worthy of Klinsmann. Hallucinatory madness. Kids were ghosting out of the gloom to peek at the monitors. It was easy to use their excitement to set up a game, a challenge.

There's a carpet pitch behind a fence in the lee of the stadium, lights of its own, a parasitical facility. The lights weren't enough to turn night into day, they spilled a sort of laboratory glow at the corners of the field. The illumination enjoyed by brain-wired beagles. We would be in our element. The flash of the Pole's camera would fuse our spastic actions with the larger drama on the other side of the great white cliff.

Most of the glue-sniffers and night casuals had drifted away from the pitch towards the circle of OB vans. They were hooked on the big match. They wanted to see the plutocrats of Man U come unstuck. Our yids and wops and darkies can stuff yours : that was the message. The two that were left, supposed brothers, were unreconstructed dysfunks, ambulant basket cases. A safe bet for the Pole. He wandered over with his bottle and a shuffle of paper to set up the challenge. A penalty shoot out. First to reach five goals. One player as the nominated goalkeeper and the other as the shooter.

The speed freak pulled on the gloves (motorcycle gauntlets) and jumped up and down, leaking gusts of white smoke. 'Yes yes yes.' He clapped his hands together. He couldn't wait to showcase his ineptitude. I couldn't afford to miss. I knew that something more than a couple of quid, and a free hit at the vodka bottle, was involved. The Pole had his arm around the kid's shoulder. The kid was mouthing his usual stream-of-consciousness rubbish. Mexicans, Indians, Mayans, sun-worshippers, snake god cannibals. Jungle bunnies with chipped profiles and a winner takes all attitude to life. These Mayans, apparently, saw football as a fate game. They played with their victims' skulls. The geometry of the court reflected a demonic cosmology. I had a bad feeling about this. Every touch of the ball was prophetic. If I hit the back of the net, so would Spurs, so would England, so would the white races, so would the order of angels. If I failed . . . Heads would surely roll.

I failed. For my first shot I concentrated on placement, not pace. I feinted left, then hit it low towards the righthand corner. The goalkeeper bluffed me. He wasn't a mover. Stood like a funeral mute, arms hanging awkwardly, until I put toe to leather. Then he sprang, anticipated me, read the flight. Tipped it, effortlessly, around the corner. Their penalty taker, a rickety beanpole who could barely stand erect without his callipers, didn't bother with a run up; smashed the ball, with no backlift, straight through the kid's arms. There was no way back. But we had to carry on to the death.

I blasted shots two and three safely into the top left corner. The same way twice, fooling nobody. The spider-monkey guessed right both times, but couldn't hold them. Their second attempt rocketed down off the post and in. The third, by some miracle, was saved. Keep diving the wrong way and sooner or later, by accident, you'll get it right.

The Pole went back to the van, fetching a black bag that, he said, contained a couple of bottles for the winners. Spurs must have tucked away their third goal, Armstrong's kneeling header, as I scored ours: top left corner again. I felt like praying. I would have been down there crawling if I could, duplicating the position of the Tottenham striker.

Could the speed freak take it to the wire? Not on his own. But the Pole had moved around directly behind the posts and his unblinking glare, red eye in the sodium-puddled darkness, threw the thin streak's concentration. He ballooned it gently into the kid's grateful grasp. See him dance and cavort. 'Come on you Irons.' He jigged and punched the air. He tried to embrace the Pole. Shove his tongue down his throat.

I pushed my luck with the final shot, aimed for my lucky corner, and had the keeper fingertip it on to the bar. Their last effort was a formality, depositing kid and ball, together, in a tangle in the corner of the net.

I was all for shaking hands, calling it an honourable draw, three apiece, and home – when the roar of the fourth Spurs goal overwhelmed us. News from a parallel universe. An adrenalin hit that was not to be denied. All or nothing. The Pole was playing with the neck of his bag. His big fists clenching and unclenching. Now the problem was the quantity of electronic interference in the air. Commentators blathering about upsets. Action replays. Slo mo distortions. Real time fractured and tormented. World Cups recalled. I kept seeing Waddle punting it high, wide and handsome. We were wired. In a mind game, we were bound to be losers: the kid with his free associating meltdown of West Ham mythology and misunderstood Mayan blood rituals, his arcane pulp images of terror, and my own crippling sense of psychogeography. His racist bile, my singular attitude towards landscape. Too much memory. We were too easily accessed. The other pair existed only in the present. Autistic innocents. Drooling but functional.

We tossed for first kick. They took it. A mishit trickled through the kid's legs. He was frozen in a drama of self-sacrifice. It was more dramatic, at this juncture, to lose heroically. Who remembers the man who hits the winning goal? But who can forget the goalkeeper's fantastic error? Gary Sprake fumbling it or the backpedalling Seaman looped from the touchline?

I travelled behind the picture of my failure. I saw the ball sailing over the bar and into the road. I heard it thump against the roof of the van. That was what the story needed and that was what I did. The full Waddle impersonation. The bandy-legged slouch. The loser's sleepwalking approach. The Marseilles scoop.

The Pole handed over cash and bottles and we walked in silence to the van. We had to get away before the real match terminated and celebrating thousands rushed out into the streets to get home to have their triumph confirmed on *Match of the Day*. To have Alan Hansen put the damper on it.

I was never much good at directions, but when the van went off the road – to avoid the worst of the traffic – and took the track through the reed beds, across the marshes, I knew we weren't heading for Hackney. The kid was in the back, blowing his bubbles, and swilling firewater. The Pole drove in silence. I couldn't see much. The fog mixed with smoke and the damp night to seal us off. When we stopped, I couldn't have guessed where we were. On the edge of the river or at the centre of a swamp. The Pole told the kid to get out and start a fire. Sat beside me, the windows wound up, headlights off, listening to the kid stumble about, whimpering that he was cold and wet, and couldn't find any dry wood. The Pole left the keys in the car and swung himself out to take control.

That's when I decided to make my run for it. When I started the engine and juddered off, blind, in the direction the van was already facing. I didn't know anything about gears, but it worked. I was moving, reeds thrashing across the windscreen. Voices behind me. It went well until the wheels stuck in the mud at the edge of the black river. Until they spun and screamed and the Pole caught up with me, claimed his forfeit.

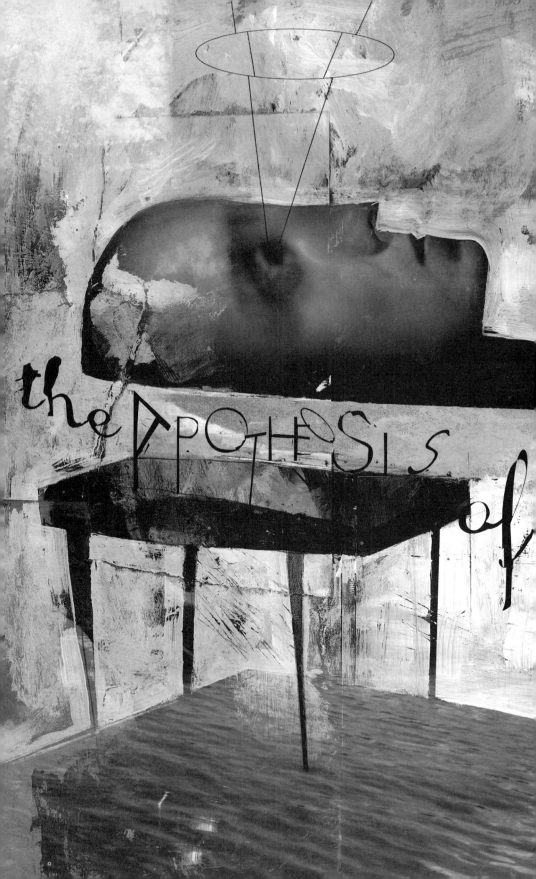

the Apothesis of

iv

lea bridge road

E5

my father used to call me his little lamb without a spot — ALFRED HITCHCOCK

the apotheosis of lea bridge road

My father used to call me his 'little lamb without a spot'
Alfred Hitchcock

*N*orton's old man floated backwards, in through the open window. Drifted over the shocked diners like a windsock. Being British, they ignored the intrusion, kept their faces in their soup plates. Hollow-cheeked, he grinned at them. Earth dribbled from his unsecured cuffs. His bald head was crowned in Virginia creeper. Norton couldn't be sure that it was his father. It might have been his own double, an ill-favoured fetch. But the floater looked too young, too chirpy. Who says it doesn't pay to have a lousy memory? Forgetfulness, Norton reckoned, was a blessing. Better than sex had ever been.

'Grass could do with a crop,' the old man gummed, gesturing towards Wanstead Flats. 'Wouldn't fancy the job myself.' He'd always preferred to visit gardens than to endure the tedium of ownership. 'Too much sodding bother.' A mob of scrawny, piss-poor pigeons were kicking up the dust on a chalk path. Lovely wet light off the gravel ponds. 'Remember now?'

Norton lost it, the vision. But the old man's voice was in his head, droning on about what he'd seen, how Walthamstow was going down the khazi. Slim brown tarts in pyjama bottoms pointing at a bird, a freak, an escaped parrot that was darting from branch to branch.

Basically, given his reduced circumstances, the fucking box in which he lived, death wasn't too bad a turn-out. He could, hand on heart, recommend it to his lad. He was getting quite fond of the muzak of the spheres. Like Mantovani on an off-day. He felt as if he'd fallen through the skirts of the trees. Down from the top of the world. Jumped without a parachute and damaged his inner ear. Sound comes slow, a cotton wool bung dipped in olive oil. He had to work to catch what was being said. Which was a bit of a laugh, after all those years training himself not to hear; bringing up marginal effects to baffle his wife's unceasing monologue.

The old man's lips move. Nothing is said.

A tidy gaff. He likes the restaurant, is amused by its presumption. A Chink noodle bar inside a mock-Tudor steakhouse. Notably pleasant. Stained wood panels, the business. He can enjoy the ambiance, on this flying visit, without fretting over the bill. Without suffering from hunger pangs. Or having to stuff his face to justify the wad he was laying out.

'Nice window table?' Why not? Belfast linen, chopsticks in a packet. Cloth the colour of a dog's dentures. Fans pinned around the walls, spread open like beheaded pigeon trophies. Ain't seen nothing to touch it. Not since he stopped going to the pictures.

Notice how the clear, bright water floats independent of the jug, honours its shape. You have to die twice, the old man thought, to appreciate the way light behaves; how it moves and trembles, the weight and form of it. We're made of light. And light is all we know. It is to light that we return.

Humans were peeping over the hedge, cheeky buggers! You'd think they'd never clocked a floater before. He was going to call Charlie Chan over to get shot of them when the bus pulled away. Get your breath back, old son. Sit tight 'til you're fit to go looking for the shop with the carpets. It's never too late. Not for the Lea Bridge Road.

Grieving and celebrating, both; the first day of summer, and Norton the walker moves out early, dew on the grass, across London Fields, Edwardian avenues of plane, dogs dropping their bundles. Mare Street: he is dazzled by the brilliance of the Town Hall steps (the brighter the building, the deeper the corruption). He's heady with release, the sense that the rest of the world, all his blood, is dead. Not a relative, a connection, living on this earth. He is free, at last. Unloved, unknown. He goes where he always goes. Narrow Way: TV rental booths, busy with bad light, debt lanterns. Caves of welfare chic schmutter. Pimp suits. The baroque infirmities of Lower Clapton Road. He works to remain positively disengaged. He lets it all drift, unedited, unreformed. He has no claim on what he sees: the London Orphan Asylum (he pauses on the far side of the locked gate) is a temple of absence. He works to shut out those clammering voices, scrubbed juveniles in bone-skin uniforms. Nothing today will persuade his notebook from his satchel. He's retired. He accepts no commissions. The phone has been ripped out and dropped in the canal. No more deadlines, no lunches. No invoices to the University of Greenwich. His target is specific, Lea Bridge Road. A journey dedicated to the memory of his father – who believed, and frequently asserted, that the road contained everything necessary for the good life. LBR was a zone of transition, a walkway between life and death. A ghost promenade, a shining path. Literally so. It blazed with cargo cult gimmicks, novelties, labour-saving devices (that were a labour to set up, and which self-destructed, with a satisfying thunderflash, at first use). Out there, still undiscovered, was the old geezer's holy grail, the shrine of the ultimate cut-price carpet. A knockdown, psychedelic Axminster that could be fitted, top and bottom, to his torpedo coffin. A Turkey fake in whose intricate curlicues he could lose himself, stories within stories. Two long years, his old man in the earth of St Pat's, Leytonstone; unvisited, under a heavy page of stone. Two years in Leytonstone was a stretch for any civilised man, quick or dead. But that was how he liked it. To be left alone. By request. Independent old sod. (Norton gifted him, now that he couldn't answer back, with all his own foibles.) His father had been brought off the street, blue in the face, loose-bowelled, with more dignity than those who make it, three parts snuffed, to Whipps Cross Hospital (where they can die in the corridor).

What was the old fool doing that day, out in the heat, hatless, loaded down with off-licence carrier bags, staggering from window to window. What was he after? What were his last words? And what was he, a tee-totaller and a notorious cheapskate, doing with all that booze? Was he going to throw his first party?

Norton gnaws fitfully on the gristle of guilt. There's a junk market down a passageway, and it's open – it has to be investigated. Most of the stalls are still sheeted, a tea urn the only area of activity. Gash video porn, disconcertingly like oversize books, covers a table; otherwise, the stock is indistinguishable from the tide-wrack you'd dredge from the fore-shore, downriver of the Thames Barrier. Hearing aids boosted from the pockets of the drowned. A child's blazer split to accommodate the shoulders of a muscular dwarf. Well-chewed plastic animals nicked from a pram.

Without enthusiasm, Norton sifts a few hundred paperbacks. They've been crammed into red trays by a reading-difficulties masochist who is punishing himself for having moved out of deleted EPs and unravelled tapes. To favour a single unit from this conglomerate requires perverse dedication. The book-objects are flavourless, sucked dry, husks of their former bombast. Deactivated. One volume sticks to his paw, threadbare black cloth, the gilt worn from its spine. *Less Than Dust* by Joseph Stamper. *The Memoirs of a Tramp*. And one that Norton does not know. Excellent. Worth 40p of anybody's money.

'Grecian statues and squashed cockroaches!' Sold! Norton has to have it. 'My bread and butter had become live-cockroach sandwiches!'

The black satchel accepts its ballast (always good to have some reading matter on board, to cover time in casualty wards, police cells, sitting on doss house steps). Encouraged, Norton heads back to the road. He is buoyant, making the best of things. Knowing from experience how soon it will go wrong.

From his vantage point at the churchyard gate, a soft-bearded vagrant targets him: 'I need a cup of tea.' Norton laughs in his face. If that were all. If the menu of wants could be reduced to such a simple demand. He fishes for a coin, the penultimate one; gives it gladly. Passes the guilt. They clasp arms like Republican comrades, returned from Spain to find that the other members of their drinking school are ghosts. The breath of the schnorrer was ripe enough to drop a cloud of midges. Add this levy to the price of the book and Norton was still in credit. The vagrant was a fine old man, one of the resources of the city, a living fossil; put some bone in the pouch of his cheeks, compost in his boots, he'd be a dead ringer for the Duke of Kent. One of them. Proof positive: there is no such thing as 'absolute poverty', except of the imagination.

Charlie Chan was putting an intolerable strain on his neck, trying to bow to a customer who was floating across the ceiling. No loss of face. The revenant wished he could say the same. When Norton's old man reached out to feel, once more, the familiar contours, his hands met. Nothing there. A masonic clasp liberated from a tombstone in St Pat's.

'Can't understand a bleedin' word.' Norton *père* drifted low over the other diners, cupping an ear. Let out of the nuthatch, that was his guess. 'Clean feeders, give 'em their due.' Only dribbling into their own sleeves. One of the loonies grins like she's shat herself. They're playing her tune. This is better than the Crazy Gang. The old man enjoyed a night up west, when the occasion arose. A musical or a double-bill. Cinema buff: anything with trains, Boche quacks, high-heel nuns, bandaged blondes. Hypodermics. Messages on steamed windows. Stick to the old formula: a doxy with spunk, a queer who can hold a tune, a bloke in a tweed jacket who can talk through clenched teeth with a pipe in his mouth.

'Never,' he boasted, 'had a takeaway in my life.' And proud to say it. Foreign muck. Time to make his way back to the Smoke. The boy. What was his name? He must be older now than I am. That's a thought.

FESTIVAL OF GRIDLOCK. A Festival at the Hindu temple closed Whipps Cross Road, Leytonstone, to traffic on Sunday as police struggled to cope with a flood of up to 15,000 worshippers.

Furious neighbours received no advance warning of the event and were overwhelmed by visitors from as far afield as Plymouth and the Midlands.

Said Tommy O'Toole, manager of the Hitchcock: 'My philosophy is that everybody in all walks of life, of all races and religions, should try and get on.

'But the organisers of this festival told none of us it was happening and had a total disregard for everybody else's feelings and needs.'

Hotel guests from abroad were unable to get to Whipps Cross Road.

THE AMERICAN CAR WASH: a cryogenic figurine draped in unseasonal oilskin twitches a robotic arm in Bates' Motel welcome. Flesh that is incapable of sweating on the hottest day. Nude beneath its fetishist wrap. A greeter with a hollow brain. Gloved hands filled with mayonnaise. Airfix skin patched from old tyres. Lip gloss. A *Texas Chainsaw Massacre* hairpiece held in place by a denim cap. Shit-eating grin.

Norton, back on the job, makes these notes. Poetry that failed its audition.

VACUUM & WINDOWS. FOAM & WASH. DONE IN MINUTES.

He's crazy with pollen. He wants to describe the city by logging the contour lines of culture. Hoardings, shop windows, newsagents' cards. And, for once, he's in the right place. Lea Bridge Road, and out. Keep moving.

A synagogue in a blitz of mustard brick. Ground poisoned by rumour: a paedophile network sacrificing kids, corpses nettled in obscurity at the back of the building. Tower block abuse. Sleeping pills, cut-price booze. Confessions no sane person can transcribe. The worst of the worst, a loop of anguish to infect poor soil. A wound that refuses to drain.

Then: open grassland, plucky with dog turds, declining towards a sluggish river. OTV. A pyramid of ex-rental sets. Traffic playbacks on many screens. Reclaimed sewage gardens on the far shore. Wild nature where it's lost its bottle. Wild nature in the terminal phase. Fenced, protected, explained away.

The Lee Valley is a prophylactic sponge soaking up grant aid. Cleansing itself, it wipes its memory bank. A new bridge. A raft of pamphlets offering walks for motorists, highlighting history that has been expunged. The Lee Valley Ice Centre is a hangar shipped in from the High Arctic. A reservation for glaciers. The temperature has turned it blue. ICE HOCKEY SUNDAY FACEOFF. 7.00 p.m.

I liked London. There's such a lot of brick, such a lot of solidified mortar, all in one place. I could shut my eyes and see uncomputable millions of men of uncountable generations all scurrying out from London, grubbing in the earth, digging out clay and sand and stone, putting it on their backs, scurrying back to London, scurrying about till they found some spot where there was no baked clay or lime-mixed sand or chisel-chipped stone, and hurriedly dumping their burden down with a satisfied grunt ere some other scurriers saw the vacant spot and dumped their burdens there.

Stamper. Norton rewarded himself for successfully crossing water by sampling a couple of lines of another man's work. Always good to find a new source from which to steal, one that no Oxbridge pedant would ever recognise.

A white bicycle lay flat on the path, a diagram to signal a designated right of way. It looked more like a warning, the outline of a recorded fatality. An invocation of disaster.

THE RIDING CENTRE. Norton was busy with his notebook, playing the cutting-edge geographer. Scrunch of horse-mouths cropping, tearing up grass in the shadow of a pylon dune. HORSE MANURE FOR SALE. £1.00 PER SACK (50p FILL YOUR OWN BAG).

Evidence. Evidence is what Norton desired. Documentation to convince himself that he was making this journey, this pilgrimage towards the ghost of his father. (What he didn't twig was that a strange female, bespectacled, hyper-hyper, twitching in post-convulsive bliss, was stalking him. That he was her narrative, the hook for a secret art event. She didn't know him and was indifferent to his published work. She thought she might take him over as a character.)

Horse imagery, Norton decided, is frequently exploited to signal a zone of upward mobility, jodhpur sex fantasies – in which the participants no longer need to be face to face. The tackle block is a social launching pad. The perfume of the hunt can lift a sagging career (i.e. MFH Jimmy Hill). Ice-skating palaces, such as the one he had just laboured past, mark the borders of the inner-city. Lee Valley water sports (post-inocula-tion) are for losers, dysfunks, petty crims. Sentimentalists, drunks, sewage surfers.

The walker can't afford leisure. He is professionally unemployed. He knows what the hobbyists will never discover, the hidden meadow behind all these sheds and play farms and enclosures. Lammas land. A green and gold patch that lifts you out of the city. (The only way he's ever going to make it.) Ambrosial air. Norton has flaked out. He spreads himself on the warm ground, screened from the effluence of the canal, the crow-speak in the cradle of overhead wires.

Memorials are constructed by subscription to ensure that we can forget with a good conscience. 'Was I part of this?' Daddy Norton tried to place himself in the ranks of the 7th Battalion, the Essex Regiment. In the 3rd East Anglian Field Ambulance. The RAMC (T). Was he one of those who gave their lives in the Great War, 1914–1918?

> *We are the dead.*
> *To you with failing hands*
> *We throw the torch;*
> *Be yours to hold it high.*

Good to be walking again, into town. Never thought it would happen. No splints, no callipers. Go anywhere he's never been. Be anything. Join the Terriers, the Inns of Court, the City Yeomanry, the Signal Squadron. 'The Home of the Devil's Own.'

He can't find himself in the shop window. 'Stand back, please. Give him air.' Like Gamages of old. You *can* go back, postmortem. Airguns, targets, tackle. THE INTERESTING SHOP. New & Used. Knives. X-Bows. Radio. Photographic Equipment. Watches. Model Trains. Curios. Lighters. Tool's. Part Exchange Welcome. No extra charge for rogue apostrophes. (Lea Bridge Road: a psychogeographical anomaly causing unconvinced apostrophes to behave like greasy butchers' hooks.)

All the kit a bedroom mercenary could lust after, hardware to counterbalance tender gatherings of porn. A *Boy's Own* checklist: Ox-Hushpower Magnum Air Guns, X-bars, Telescopic 4×40mm sights, 'Fox' recoiless (sic) Self-Assembly Air Rifles. 'Interesting' is a euphemism for deadly, deathdelivering, mean. All the things young Norton loved, saved for, got. They killed you. A sleek crow perched on an apple-tree. An antique BSA that had lost its pop. The boy took aim, fired. The bird was so much bigger when it flapped on the stone path, blood dripping from its eye. He left the old man to do the dirty work, smash its head. Muck on the spade. 'Must have flown into a telephone wire, Dad.'

As Norton the walker climbs, N.N.E, the diesel fug rises with him; the Lea Bridge Road has become a hologram of *Exchange & Mart*, a virtual reality consumer catalogue. Everything you didn't know you needed and then some. All the major specialists in obscurity.

CAR GRAPHICS MADE TO ORDER. MAGNETIC VEHICLE SIGNS. Outside the first newsagent, a billboard: AUTO TRADER. The poor old sandwichman, the ambulant advertisement, has been pensioned off. Exit left, Joseph Stamper.

Slowly you parade along, lolling and rolling from one side to the other at every step as a paddle-boat in a swell. Going along a main street in the gutter at one side, crossing at the end of the street, and coming back along the gutter at the other side. Traffic whizzing by you within an inch; despised and ignored for the most part by the pedestrians, it is the most dead-alive business man has ever devised, like to that of the dull-eyed bullock yoked to an ancient pumping windlass.

Furtive now, Norton cuffs the sweat from his eyes, takes note of the collage of touts' cards in the newsagent's window. He's a lurker. A punter without a pot to piss in (one coin left). He's a freak without a legitimate fetish. He's clocked (as he imagines it) by properly purposed citizens. (And, as he does not imagine it, by the woman with the beaver hat. And the camera.)

Scratch, scratch, scratch. The biro drills at the notebook, his ever-expanding catalogue of urban ephemera. PONDERS END SAUNA MASSAGE. SOUTH AMERICAN. SEXI TONI (ALL SERVICES). FLUFFY, HALF-PERSIAN. BUSTY CARIBBEAN. NIKOLE – DISCREET MASSAGE. 38″ MASSAGE BY BLACK GIRLS (QUIET LOCAL). SWEET KITTENS GIVEN AWAY.

Black limos, three of them in convoy. Roof-top flower gardens. They slide effortlessly uphill. A single cab weaving as it tracks them. Can't match the panther-power of the deluxe meat wagons. The air-conditioned ride of a lifetime. A young black kid saunters into the road to gob on the taxi's windscreen.

Norton transcribes everything. Meaningless occurrences. The trivia of the real. And, by his actions, creates fiction. Once written, it cannot be trusted. Not even the boasts in shop windows.

OVERALLS: WE ARE THE CHEAPEST. NEW & RECONDITIONED BOILER SUITS. END OF LINE BOILER SUITS £10.50. CHEF'S TROUSERS £8. NURSES DRESS £10.

Emmanuel Church (CHRIST IS SPOKEN HERE).

Time to blow the last coin on a coffee. The Roma. His passage to the grease caff is blocked by a grinning plaster chef (The Captain's Table), who has evidently been kitted out, at a discount, by the overall shop. The chef's beard is a clump of ginger pubic clippings painted with glue. Moustache: the rust on a file. The right hand masks the nipple in a masonic gesture that leads the eye towards a lidded silver platter (large enough to contain the parboiled head of Sir Edward Heath).

In the cool of the caff, there's a handbell to summon the catering operative. RING FOR SERVICE. But with how much enthusiasm? It's the mid-morning lull, between shifts; complimentary copy of the *Sun* folded away. The formica shines in scarlet streaks, where the surface has received its first wipe. Damp catches the lounger's elbow, a trapezoid trap, a windscreen smeared by a single blade. The local crumblies, crouching low to avoid being noticed (and culled), are beginning to manifest; to appear at reserved tables without passing through the door. They eke out a shared cuppa and stare at the street.

Norton finds the courage to lift the bell, the faintest of tinkles. On the instant, unprepared, he has to take a decision about the size of cup he requires. He risks the large, the porcelain spittoon. Feels obliged, back at his table, to pay tribute (in the black notebook) to the singular method by which his coffee has been prepared. A squirt of water, a generous measure of milk. Steam hosed into the mix. Only then, the brew hissing and spitting, is dark powder seeded on the surface; a sinking pyramid (like the choc-dust flourish in Frith Street cappuccino). It's left to the punter to do his own stirring. Or to gag on the tarry lump and take the diluted milk straight. As a chaser. The experience, Norton wrote, was quite acceptable. The lower depths, as he sucked the dregs, were cold as yesterday's custard.

Now comes the shock, the heart flutter. A streetwoman bangs a card down on his table and grins in his face. Then she's gone. He knows he's going to regret it, but curiosity gets the better of him. He reads (before he tears the art prompt into microscopic fragments): 'So that you may know that I am but not who I am.'

'I'll never find the boy now,' said Norton's dad. The street had grown and the city was further away. Last he knew, his firstborn had found employment, in a borrowed kipper tie, hawking rubbish door-to-door. Car maintenance kits to palsied pensioners. Bum bags to darkies in discount stores. Got a nerve, give him that. Keep it up another six months and they'll take him on the firm.

NEW & USED WHEELCHAIRS & SCOOTERS. Know what? The old man

discovered that he possessed the ability, without breaking wind, to make the golf carts shunt – by psychic energy. Disinterested consciousness, imagine that. The shopman sprints outside, all his electricals rocking and rolling like moored cabin-cruisers hit by a tidal wave. He smiles thinly, revenge in his eyes. He'd like to crucify a few blacks, torch a Chinese take-away. But he suspects a Jeremy Beadle scam and is determined, at all costs, to appear game. To give the cameras their pound of flesh.

LEYTON LEISURE LAGOON. THE FAST TANNING CENTRE. Lea Bridge Road: all centres and no circumference. Metaphors in love with themselves. Like those ladders propping up the tall thin shop. Drew, Clark & Co. By Appointment to Her Majesty the Queen Mother, Manufacturers of Ladders. (So useful for midnight prowlers, solicitors of crested cigarettes.)

After the shooting of George Cornell (fat bullet, fatter target), this was where Ron Kray hid out: above a butcher's shop. Still there. The shop, not Ron. Norton is there too, brooding on this future past. An exchange of nightmares, murderer and murderee. Powder burns on the ceiling. Dark bottles on a bamboo bar. Plaster scurfing the net-filtered light. Bandages around the eyes. They hurt. Ron's short of company. His whereabouts a secret half the faces in East London are forced to share. Fear of blindness. Spit turns to acid, damages the veneer. He is tainted by association with that lowlife name, the Beggar.

Cornell's first soul splinters on impact. His second soul takes flight, blue smoke of sunshock. His name-soul is cursed in repetition. It struggles to define itself above the gossip of hair-clippers on bull necks. Liquid soap and linoleum. Bent dog ends smouldering in the cat's dish. Plastic-shrouded furniture. Food sent up on a tray. The convalescence of serial killers.

The Bakers Arms is a significant bus stop. A destination respected throughout the length and breadth of Hackney. Norton tries to postpone the finish, the failure of his quest, by checking out a charity shop. SENSE (Eyes & Ears of Deaf-Blind People). He forces his way into an unfumigated wardrobe: carpet slippers, suits from stiffs, brogues riveted in braille. Shelves of books packed so tight that no single volume can be removed. The volunteer stacker, who is searching for a particular author (and also for something to do), has no formal training, no library skills. Books are sorted according to size and colour. The rationale goes like this: top shelf for hardbacks, second for paperbacks, third for Mills & Boon, and the rest, the unsorted juvenilia, in boxes on the floor.

'It's too easy being miserable. Anyone can get stuck into a good book. Who was it you wanted again, dear?'

'Lena Kennedy. Some people can use words. She can. And she's from round here. Gets it right every time.'

'Good then are they?'

'I'm telling you, you could be there.'

'We are, dear, some of us. Bleedin' stuck 'ere. That's the trouble.'

COMPETITIVE INSURANCE/DENTURE REPAIRS (QUICK SERVICE).
ORTHOPEDIC BED CENTRE. Royal Dolphin: the Traditional Sunday Lunch. Spaghetti Bolognese, Avocado Vinegrette (sic), Fried Squid, Chicken Helenic with Salad, Deserts from the Trolley, Coffee & Mints. £9.50 + 10 pc service.

Norton's too far from Mare Street. He gets the first dangerous whiff of Epping Forest and starts to lose his shape. These terrraces can hardly be called London. A couple more miles and Norton would be a smear of gas. Whipps Cross roundabout. Residential care for the incontinent. VICTORIAN FIREPLACES MADE TO ORDER. LOBSTERS. NEW SEASON COOKED EELS.

Here is greenery he can't ignore. He should turn for home before it's too late. Sunlight skating on the surface of gravel ponds. Groves sacred to extremes of asceticism and perversion. He remembers a forensic snuff-shot. A transvestite in black underwear who miscalculated a breeze block suspension. High Tory auto-erotic asphyxiation. 'These deaths are accidental; and not to be confused with suicide.' Liberties of the forest.

In a shimmering cloak of waterlight, Norton backs through the open door. Through a curtain of poison ivy. Cool as an igloo in here. He carries his drink across to the Alfred Hitchcock shrine, a wall of production stills in formaldehyde colours. A terrified blonde in a choke of birds. Photocopied newspaper interviews.

My secret? Put an ordinary man in an extraordinary situation and you have full audience participation.

Cigar smoke. Iced Pils. Let the photographs, the film frames, tell their own story. Voyeurism. Rituals of programmed violence. The memory spools unravelling at both ends of the Lea Bridge Road: the Hitchcock pub and the London Orphan Asylum. Norton walking towards Norton.

A coven of geriatrics infiltrate the bar space, blinking, as they step down out of the harsh sunlight. Are they all dead? They are blustering, unsure of their status. Grey hair, reprieved suits. Mothballs and cheap cologne. It was hardly worth the return fare from the graveyard. But they are light-hearted, don't need the booze: it wasn't them, not this time. Some other sod bought it. They saw him folded into the ground.

Norton didn't go to the funeral. He'd been there too often before. One jewelled droplet of semen hanging from the granite ledge of the cross. He wouldn't find, among those acres of stone angels, the place where they'd dumped his old man. It was a fruitless excursion. Never to look again into those cold blue eyes. Or place his hand over that open mouth. Stroke the bristled cheek. His dad wouldn't have wanted it, not now, not then.

It was too late. He knew, lifting the glass to his head, rolling it against a rising fever, that he had become everything that his father once was.

Norton Senior is content. Intricate patterns that would unhinge a less determined mind, colours that put the rainbow to shame. At last, at the death, the carpet shop! He'd searched for it all his life. Bugger the expense. A carpet woven expressly for him, his spiritual autobiography. A twist in the weave like a bird's neck, a parrot in flight. Granddad kept one for years. Evil fucker, temper like a woman. Spiteful. You could see it in his eye. The soul of some Peruvian snake-priest trapped there.

The empty cage lasted longer than his dad's dad. Rusting away in the garage on a heap of coal. You should be crowing, son. Rid of the lot of us. Pick any thread and trace it to a finish. If you've got the bottle. See how it ends.

He saw his son in the window. He couldn't turn away. It wasn't too late, not yet. Then the pain rolled into a great black ball and wedged in his throat. He fell to the ground, hearing every word they said. 'For God's sake, give him air. Will someone please send for an ambulance?'

NO MORE YOGA OF THE NIGHT—

CLUB

V

When you're dead you can't talk. Yet you feel like you could. - Gregory Corso

no more yoga of the night club

When you're dead you can't talk
Yet you feel like you could
Gregory Corso

He was supposed to pick up the Bubble on Queens-bridge Road, over the hump, down by the Acorn, then go directly to the gaff of a man named Norton and waste him. Norton, not the Bubble. Only the colonel, he didn't say 'waste'. He wouldn't show hisself up. He said, 'It's on Norton tonight. There's a oncer in it, Jack. You'll be doing yourself a favour, son.'

But that was never Jack's forte, doing hisself favours. Not his style. Jack was well-known for it, being a cast-iron irritant. A poker in the fundament. Jack didn't so much get up your nose, he potholed your hooter, crampons, icepick and steel-capped Doc Martens. Contrariness, that's what he specialised in. And he wasn't all mouth. Jack was the perfect antidote to bullshit. He was far worse than he knew. Blow off your kneecaps, tear out your Adam's apple, stomp your kidneys, but he'd never hold it against you. Clock you at the bar, your glass half full, he'd help you drain it. Jack had no time for barbers, tailors, all that patriotic cobblers about Churchill and Lawrence of poxy Arabia. 'Bunch of poofs, Tone. Towelhead slags.' Spot a dewy-eyed Alsatian asleep on the doorstep and Jack would give it a good kicking. Pussy cats turned into oven gloves when he passed them on the stairs. He walked in his own force field: reverse magnetism. He hated with good heart, lived on speed and fags still wet from some other geezer's carious cakehole. I never once caught him going without, never saw him buy his own, putting his hand in his pocket. The city, Jack considered, owed him a living. He had as much right as any man to gob on the cobble-stones. Leave your wad lying around in your trousers and Jack would share it. He was like that, a legend among his own. He emptied pubs quicker than Barbara Cartland getting her kit off, quicker than karaoke night with the Donoghue brothers from Silvertown. You could chart his progress between Haggerston and Newington Green, up Green Lanes to Finsbury Park, like a tidal wave, a tornado, leaving boozers with their doors off, furniture in the air, blood, smoke, and plaster snowstorms.

Jack was a chaos punter, everything was *now*. Time was no hindrance. Jack felt it, he did it. Look at those other lizards, the stern mugs in the nightclub group shots: fated. Printed with death. Inked over with a sense of their own importance. Destiny, for those berks, was getting rat-arsed with Judy Garland, bunging a couple of grand into Johnnie Ray's bottom drawer. History was calibrated in the measurement of Ronnie Kray's inside leg. They stuttered the temporal flow. Tried to dam the stream. Wait. Pause. Let this single moment be the one and all. See the wicked cut of that collar, see the handshake with Sonny Liston. See us share the frame with George Raft. Posers. Window dressers. Jack wasn't going to doff his hat for David Bailey. Jack liked to drink without witnesses, liked to stay off the map, a pub with a couple of entrances, across the precinct from a betting shop. Jack patronised establishments that carried big slates and no chalk. The first sign of an elevated stage, a bit of greenery, a sepia memento of old London, and he was on his toes. He was convivial, but didn't care for society. The Bubble was as handy as anyone for keeping the drinks coming. If he wanted Jack to make up the numbers for a bit of business, that was all right too. Jack was never what you could call socially promiscuous. He didn't speak of Tone as a mate. He did what he had to do, he rubbed along. He'd go over the pavement with a shooter, or take a run up the motorway to Birmingham to put the frighteners on some bent motor trader. He was easy, but he wasn't short of temperament. Given the provocation, he'd reduce any premises to rubble. A Paki had lipped him once, back of Scriven Street, when he questioned the mark up on a packet of gaspers. Jack torched the gaff. Down Hackney Road they still talked about the time when Jack, dissatisfied by the bite of the vinegar, lobbed a moggy into the fish fryer. All the faces acknowledged, he had a very particular sense of humour.

But Jack had his principles too. He'd never sit down to drink. And that's where he got hisself into bother. The Carpenters Arms ran to rules of etiquette as tight as a Mason's lodge, a gathering of samurai. In the normal run of things, Jack kept well clear. But that night, as chance would have it, Tone had the wheels. Tone was picking up change introducing a pair of brothers from West London to the Twins. A fucking genealogist of the inner city. He was putting them straight, adjusting his mirror so they could correct any stray hair, flakes of skull-snow on the padded shoulders. The boys wanted to piss first, against the church railings, so they wouldn't have to show theirselves up when they got indoors. Jack, he didn't like this. He was all for following them out and sticking their Brylcreem'd heads through the bars, getting their slacks down for a good striping. 'Cunts,' Jack said. 'Making cunts of theirselves for a pair of fat poofs.' Jack held that on a good night out, you never, *never*, micturated. 'Go to the khazi when you've had a skinful and you lay yourself open. They'll come at you five-handed and you're fucked, son.' Jack was a master of the zen art of water retention. He sweated the alcohol out. That was his theory: muffler, leather waistcoat, cardi, sports jacket, tweed overcoat, trilby. In the close confinement of the tap-room, he sweated buckets. He was always rubbing his eyes, mopping his greasy brow with a trailing cuff. The look of the man was an affront to the sartorial standards the Twins always strove to uphold. Ron, in the early days, was Reg's mirror. Reg – hair, shoulders, whistle – was the spit of Edmund Purdom.

Jack never was one to gauge the temperature of an event. His entrance, knocking Ron's favourite dwarf off of his stool, elbowing drinkers, setting a grubby suede shoe on the rail and asking one of the henchmen to sniff it for dog shit, was a disaster. The colonel liked to have space around him, the length of a cutlass, a bayonetsworth of privatised air. You kept clear, unless you was invited to link arms with Ronnie Fraser or Victor Spinetti, squeeze mits with Terry Spinks, give your backing to Babs Windsor for a photograph. They had more pictures plastered on the wall than the National Gallery. Ranks of bottles on the table. Celebrities paying their respects. Another era entirely. Know-nothings talk about the class system breaking down, old Etonian chancers sharing a half with badly-wired psychopaths, blisters on their knuckles. Taffeta crooners talking horse-flesh with bent peers. Gangsters trading rent boys with unfrocked cabinet ministers. All bollocks! Caste was as rigidly enforced as at Versailles. Louis XIV was a fucking *laissez-faire* amateur compared to the colonel. Even the colonel's monkey wiped his arse with crested two-ply tissue.

The colonel's stretch of the bar, teak polished like a coffin, was inviolate. No other word for it. One of his lads ducking in from time to time to keep the menthol-tip aglow, or to slide another gin into reach, that was all the movement he tolerated. And here's Jack, hat perched on his ears indoors, like a potato basher. Like he's just come in from the cowshed, his corduroys held up with creosoted twine. 'Arright, colonel? Have one with me. Tone, get a proper drink in for Ron. Some fucking peasant's given the poor sod a poof's glass. Drink that and he'll smear his lipstick. Fetch him a whiskey, Tone. And make mine a double.'

The colonel never moves. He don't turn round, nothing. All the rabbit stops. The big freeze. Eyeballs on stalks, like their heads was being squeezed in a vice. The colonel's neck. A vein the size of your thumb, see it pumping. Jack is totally unaware of the mayhem, the potential mayhem, he has initiated. If Jack had more teeth he'd be whistling. Shirt-tails out like a dosser, he starts scratching his bollocks. There's a sound like dice rattling in a plastic beaker. It's the brothers from West London, their knees knocking. All they wanted was the photograph, something to frame in the Portakabin, the visible proof of their connections. Now they were webbed up in a treason trial. Tongues like old rope. Mouths burnt with the scorch of it, time running backwards. What they saw, all of them in that room, was the finish. The blood and cartilage on the carpet. Tone with a red can soaking the furniture with petrol. The house going off like a fire bomb. Jack gazing up at them out of wet concrete. His hat blowing away across the Swanscombe Marshes, under the bridge. They saw theirselves, names, ages, petty deceptions, spread across the tabloids. In their bowels they knew the dyspepsia of foreknowledge. Jack, oblivious, chucked back his Irish.

The route Jack's body took was like a fucking mantra: Evering Road, Lower Clapton Road, Narrow Way, Mare Street, Cambridge Heath Road, Commercial Road, East India Dock Road and through the tunnel, under the river. Get shot of this over-articulate corpse. Leave it to Freddie Foreman. Tone had sweated his jacket. You could ring the Bubble out. He was memorising the geography of an event which had not yet happened, which might never happen. He was back here, greyer, hidden behind designer bins, giving it the old sincerity in an empty boozer. He was here in the morning, for fuck's sake! Telling the story to a TV crew. Narrow Way. The words stuck in his throat. He looked down at his own hand and he couldn't get it into focus. It was a ghost hand. It was like his fucking hand had died and the rest of him still attached to it. His hand was moving through so many positions in one instant of time. A white fern. A sommelier with the terminal shakes.

'It's on Norton tonight. You'll be doing yourself a favour, Jack. Use Tone's motor.' And the colonel peeled off a couple of notes from a roll. He might be royalty, he might not like spoiling the hang of a suit, but he wasn't soft in the head. Not where readies were concerned. He carried his own wad. Like a hard paper cock pressing against his ice heart.

Jack didn't touch the notes. He put his glass down on top of them, let them lie like a Gulbenkian tip, a backhander. Nodded at the guvnor. 'Do us a triple, Stan.' Ron would never have tolerated a brass behind the bar, too much rabbit. Working women were nothing but fucking trouble. But Jack was in no hurry. Norton? Never heard of the cunt.

Now they're on the road. It's daylight. Another day, the same day. They're looking for a geezer neither of them know. Norton? Sounds like a solicitor, half a bent brief. They're supposed to kill him, but the Bubble reckons that's taking the colonel too literal. Ron don't know his own mind when he's had a skinful. A good slap'll do it. Shove his poxy hands in the door, crack a few knuckles. A dig. A poke. Use the tyre lever. Kill him for a oncer?

Leave it out. What's he done anyhow? Fuck knows. Jack nodding off, needs something to keep him on the job. The Bubble smokes a bit of grass, that's the size of it, he's no junkie. Jack'll do anything. Jack's game. Known for it. The early sunlight, a stranger to the man in the hat, flirts with his stitches. Warmth coming through the curved screen polishes the razor scars on Jack's boat. Jack's always gone private, handled his own medicals. A kitchen scissors and a pair of the old woman's tweezers. Like digging maggots out of wet toffee. Terrible to watch, if you walked in on it unexpected, but Jack was impervious to pain. Anaesthetised by letting a little blood into his alcohol. Tone watched him take the tip off his finger, trying to carve a cottage loaf. Not a word, not a fucking twitch of the lip. The morning's radiance heated the plastic threads in his cheek, brought him back to where he was.

Where *was* he? This wasn't fit ground for a whiteman. This was the fucking jungle. You'd need Tonto to take you round, a darkie who could read rhino shit. They tried Kinder Street but it wasn't there. Some cunt had nicked the lot, every bleeding stone of it. Sly Street weren't even a tin sign. Rubble and corrugated iron blowing in the wind. Jack wouldn't climb out of the motor. He spun the wheels, reversed sharpish out of a dead end. In his own mind, he did. In the film of it. He could feel the wheel in one hand and the lovely cool metal of a shooter in the other. London settled on its proper axis. He *thought* the Jag into where it was, Paki town. Bits that ain't on the map. Jack floated, inside the motor, down streets he'd never seen in his life. Air was water. So was the colonel. A bag of water in mohair casing. Gin and water. A bag of piss. Eau de Cologne and pure sewage. There's a river in Detroit, one of the boys who came over told Tone, that's all industrial crap, from the car factories, toxic shit. Your foot'd fall off if you tried to paddle. But they pour blue dye into this river every day. And it comes out like the Venice honeymoon of your dreams. That's the colonel, that's Ron. Dyed shit. Green skin and pockets stuffed with deceased carnations.

But, truth to tell, Jack wasn't driving. He wasn't in charge. He was there all right, in the driver's seat, the Englishman's position, righthand side for right-minded citizen. Jack the democrat, English as roast beef. Jack the storybook adventurer, working through the karma of his Jock surname. Jack keeping up standards among a bunch of wops, dagos, pikies. Jack on the tenter grounds. Jack with the whiff of the river in his nostrils. He wound down the window, none of that electric bollocks, a decent motor that would never go out of fashion. A hearse. A scarlet hearse. A motor that had travelled through time. A sixties jam jar still active, revisiting the streets of shame. A revenant wagon. A transporter of dead men. A limbo shuttle.

What if, Jack thought, we was a future nightmare? What if the things we done couldn't be shifted? Knocked out of the book. What if we was the aliens some stupid bastard saw? A fireball over Wapping? The motor like a disk of red light? Still cruising for human meat, still on active service. Moving without touching the pedals. This was an export Jag, exported inwards, straight out of the packing case. Straight out of Tilbury. A shnide Jag with upholstery that would never now be too hot to touch on the desert road to Palm Springs. That would never feel the imprint of bare-arsed Californian crumpet. The Bubble was the chauffeur. The motor was in the charge of a left-footer, hung with a voodoo of plastic saints, pierced hearts, prayer beads that glowed like droplets of transcendent blood. Tone drove, took the dictation of Jack's diseased psyche.

He could see it all with his eyes shut. The air was sweet. His nose pricked, he sneezed. He was stretched out in a meadow. Out of it completely. Hung over without the headache. Breath like violets. He blew into his cupped hand, sniffed it. He couldn't get comfortable. He rolled and twisted. His mouth felt as if he'd been gargling with granite chips. He tried to spit. His shirt was soaked. Only blood. A nick, a scratch. Lifted his hands to shade the splintering sun. Which end of the day? A new beginning. Roofs and church towers and flashes from distant glass pyramids. Was this London? Not that he recognised. A ribbon of blue townscape on the far side of the water. A meadow. He liked that word. A field in the city. In close proximity. A field that they hadn't noticed. Jack lifted, floated off. Went with the gentle zephyr that ruffled the grove of trees. He fancied shade, a log to rest his back. He'd sit there, watching the insects in the old dry wood.

Jack let the bleached grass run back into the dust on the windscreen. Let the meadow bleed into the wasteground they were bumping across, dogs guarding a wrapped tower block. Jack's hand found the reassurance of metal. In the meadow was a metal disk. Jack traced the letters with his fingers. *Broads 70c Silent Knight*. A plate that had dropped from nowhere into this field. A manhole cover. A lid securing the plunge into who knows what depths. The rush of black water. Had Jack pissed hisself? Being, at one time, in two places? He shook out a couple of pills, took a flat bottle from his pocket, washed them down with the fiery dregs. Chucked the bottle from the window.

In the meadow, exposed in all that hot space. Jack heard the sound of breaking glass, glass shattering on London stone. A pair of pillowcase hags shuffled along, eyes on the ground, determined not to see what was happening in front of them. Don't get involved with heretic business. Stay inside your bin bags. They stared straight through Jack and the motor. The Bubble's head was on fire. He was going through the Piccadillys like they was about to be rationed. Like he could see something in the smoke, the genie at the bottom of the bottle. Like he knew what would happen if Jack caught him. Jack would nick the fucking packet. Remember the night he'd gone with Jack to the turnout at Highbury Corner? 'Wanna come along,' Jack said, 'and make one with me?'

An old slapper, who in her prime had gigged at the Palladium, was throwing her annual comeback. The gaff, a Paddy toilet, was packed. Nothing to do with her, though some of the chaps thought it would be a hoot to watch her croak. But her feller, a TV ponce, a safari suit who was about to dump the cow, take a better offer for his services, done a deal with the micks, to cop for the bar bill. And the micks let in a mob of their own, hair licked with sugar water, bum-freezer church suits, hobnail boots. All the flakes in the borough, all the riffraff out of Chapel Street, all the potato bashers down from Archway, are up for it. Jack was a prince on this turf. He swaggered through the swing doors like John Wayne doing the double hernia tango, knees stapled together, rolling. The Bubble shadows him, maintains his distance, wop-slick, Dean Martin. You couldn't call Jack legless, not if you didn't want a dig. Jack was so pissed his boots squelched.

He'd had some bother that afternoon, down the Mildmay, done his wad, stood at the bar shouting his mouth off. Bennie One-Ear was trying to interest him in a barrel of sausage casings, skins in brine. He was getting on Jack's wick, explaining how the profit was as good as hoisting a vanload of ciggies, without the risk. 'There's no security, Jack,' he'd say.

'Fuck security.'

'Be smart, Jack, play percentages.'

'Fuck percentages, you mutt cunt.' Back and forth. Jack trying to keep up with the card at Kempton, the colour on the telly shot to buggery.

In the finish, Jack fucks off out of it, they won't serve him no more. The guvnor says to Bennie, he's never seen Jack go so quiet. He's about to lock up, get out the cards, when Jack staggers in with something sticking out of his cheek. The state of him, a purple-arse baboon from Bongobongo land! Like he's bunked off from Stan Baker's *Zulu*. 'Sausage casings, you cunts? I'll fill your fucking sausage casings.'

He's got a bin bag stuffed with cashmoney. He tips it over the bar. 'Enough for you, Bennie, you mouthy cunt? Get 'em in 'Arry. You gone mutton like the fucking yid?' And he pulls a shotgun out from under his jacket and blasts the ceiling. Plaster fallout dropping in their beer the rest of the afternoon. They pissed theirselves, the way Jack told it. He gone over the road to the betting shop, in the backroom, straightened the manager, says he's collecting for the Twins. Puts them in for it. On his way through one of the kids who's supposed to be minding the float has a pop at Jack. Don't know him, never seen him before. He ain't got a tool, so he sticks a biro in Jack's boat. Like a fucking porcupine. Blood and blue ink spouting together. A Glasgow kiss done the kid's nose. He's on the deck whimpering. Jack's emptying the till, walks out with the guvnor's blunderbuss.

By the time Tone steers him down Highbury, Jack's choice. He's got a black ring on his cheek, like some quack's tried to mark up the exit wound. His shirt is decorated with phlegm, spew, and five kinds of blood, one of them his own. There's a cocktail of booze soaked into his sports coat. He never wears no tie, but somewhere that afternoon he's picked up two of the cunts. He's sweating like a stallion. All the acid, the waste he won't piss away. He's hot for it. The speed's slowing down and the vodka's got a clear run into his rage centres. Red eyes? No pupil left. Burning coals. He's as twisted as a cyclone. Ready to unwind.

When the old crow, she's drunker than Jack, falls on the stage, the gaff goes quiet. No one wants to give the first catcall. It would be like mocking the dead. She's your best mate's mum, more wrinkles than Club Row. Yellow-toothed sheep dressed as fucking rack of lamb. Half of Shirley Bassey's dress riding around her lard arse, mascara wasted like the close of Judy Garland's final performance. She's got her arm around the mike to keep herself up. When she detaches it, the red-faced labouring men don't know where to look. You'd think she's made a grab for a dildo. It's a treat for a queeny audience, a drama diva coming apart at the seams. But they've got the wrong crowd in. A couple of murdered torch songs get a ripple of applause, then she goes for the big saccharine close. Old Shep. Dead Elvis. Saint Elvis. A dog song. Arthritic knuckles knot around pint pots. Rosary beads are juggled like gallstones. Mildewed sleeves mop up the tears. The boiler's old man is up on his toes, he's off out of it. He'll take Lew Grade's starvation wages. Any drudgery is better than this. He'd rather sit through an eternity of Shirley MacLaine's rebirthing experiences.

Gobsmacked, Tone watched the curds oozing out of the side of Jack's mouth. Meltdown. It was a race with the froth climaxing on the bottle in his fist. The instant before he threw it. Into the band. It missed the singer. She was too far gone to notice. Blinded by a landslip of eye shadow, ill-fitting and mismatched contact lenses. Jack lobbed an empty. They were geriatrics, the musicians. Derby and Joan, bar mitzvah occasionals. Ruffed-shirt and pacemaker. Dentures clacking against brass. A drummer who chased the beat like an old flame. They didn't want trouble. They downed tools and left her to it. An a cappella nightmare, glass scratching slate. Circumcision of the throat. Vocal chords tight as a ligature. Autoerotic self-strangulation. Dying and coming. The wet squeak of a fork puncturing a rubber chicken.

Jack picked up a metal ashtray. It caught the side of her head. She swayed, tried to remember where she was, fell from the stage. Her shoulder straps gave up the unequal struggle. All of her, scented, hysterical, in and out of her spangles, cascaded on to the lap of a righteous Kerryman. Twelve stone of unrequired lap dancer, Old Shep's shaggy corpse not yet cold in her arms.

The micks have tried to give the poxy toilet a bit of class for the evening, candles in bottles, a bunch of weeds in a vase, if you're lucky. Jack marched over to the bird and pulled her up, brushed her down. Tried to pour meadowsweets and water into her bosom. All that whalebone and talcum powder. Had his arm in, right to the elbow, before the paddies landed on his back. They couldn't untangle them, a marriage consummated in the black museum.

The Bubble made a strategic withdrawal, went for the motor. Took the plastic sheeting out of the boot and covered the seats. Jack was a mess when they tired of it, the punishment beating. Their clumsy homage to a great trooper. There'd be more home-knitting when Jack got indoors, when his old woman copped hold of what was left of him. He'd be up half the night with a needle sewing his face together. When the colonel hears about this turnout, he'll shit hisself. An embolism on the spot. Two rules Ron lives by: respect for others and the sanctity of showbiz. What would he make of Jack, flies open, elbows on the formica, shouting for his old woman to get the breakfast on the table? Three thirty in the morning and he wants the full fucking fry. How could the colonel repair the damage? A star who has touched the gloved hand of Princess Margaret as good as raped on the floor of a club under his benevolent protection. Diabolical liberty don't begin to cover it.

Hessell Street. Take my word for it, you don't want to go down there. Nothing to work with but a name you can't put a face to. Norton. Notron. Not Ron. When the Bubble's nervous, he runs words backwards. Can't hardly speak fucking English in the first place. His old man's been over here since the war and he ain't never got out of the kebab kitchen. A drink of a Christmas morning in the Belgrave Arms, that's the length of it. Not Ron. Tone's got a bad feeling about this one, a geezer defined by his negative capabilities. Ron's antibody. Naked, scrotum-tightening terror's better than a course in the Open University. He's thinking thoughts so occult you could classify them as philosophy.

Jack's nodded off, dreaming of being asleep. Dreaming of shunting a Jag down Hessell Street, a place he would never go as a mortal soul. 'Like Tangier down there,' he muttered. 'Like the fucking bazaar. Ali Baba land. Food you wouldn't feed your arsehole. We're the cunts. The colonel's got us in a fucking Punch and Judy show, Tone.'

Amazon Street, a poxy tributary. Hard to believe a whiteman would live here. Who said Norton was *white*? Who said Norton exists? There's no record of him. The colonel's got them chasing shadows. He's decoyed them into bandit country. Each street, each stinking alley, worse than the last. Jack jumps out of the motor, up the steps, into a shop that's more like a cave, a hole in the wall. Flies blanketing pinky blue meat. Bringing flesh lumps back to life. A wool of buzzing noise. 'Oi, Sabu. Know where find Norton? Savvy?' He pelts the old man with green tomatoes. He tips out sacks of bright spices, overturns golden yellow heaps – as if Norton should be there, squatting behind the rice barrier.

Norton. He could be any fucking shape or size, any age. You'd never go on Ron's powers of description. The colonel thought of Eric the Horse from Walthamstow, when he was properly cased up, as having looks 'synonymous' with Gary Cooper. And this a mug what can't hardly get his chin on the bar, more arm than a spider, ears like dinner plates, two hairs fighting it out on the top of his head, and a hooter with less altitude than the fucking fens. Call him Lon Chaney and you'd be flattering him. Ron could never see the man behind the tailoring.

'We've knocked out the drinking money, let's fuck off out of it.' Jack folded his arms, shut his eyes, let the Bubble graft an exit. It was one of those days when the clouds had poodled into each other, no sky worth speaking of, a tin lid on the city. You're sweating inside a poxy tent. That and the stink of alien vegetables, cat piss, cardamom. Tone was claustro-phobic, agoraphobic. The lot. That afternoon, he was allergic to life. And it showed. No fucker watching him and his face gave it away. A condemned man waiting for the fake cupboard at the back of the cell to slide away, waiting gratefully for the cloth hood. The step into the dark.

Jack was restless. The waking dream was crap. He fancied more pills. He told Tone to cut back through Spitalfields, shoot into the Golden Heart. His fresh scars, the attempts he'd made to dig the cat gut out of his cheek, were gleaming. He looked like sunset over Willesden Junction.

Nobody knows Jack's old lady. Jack keeps her well out of it. She keeps out of it herself. The kids, she rules them, runs them. Jack knows his place, kitchen table, and, on occasion, out back with a football and a small red tricycle. Indoors, Jack's a benevolent clown, a familiar stranger. Jack is unbuttoned. He don't need to assert his eccentricity. He don't need to piss in his own grate. The kids tolerate Jack. A good provider, his pockets heavy with change. The old woman can have any gear she wants. 'Pick a label,' Jack says. 'For fuck's sake.' Shirley, down Hoxton, smart salt, would boost to order. She had Vi Kray turned out like Lady Onassis, like Oscar night in Tinseltown. Shirley *lived* in Harrods, she did, closed the fur department on her own. More expensive commodities had been stuffed down her knickers than you'd fit Kurds in a sweatshop. But Jack's old woman she don't want to know. 'I can dress myself, Jack.' They understood one another, mutual distrust. Different species entirely. They rowed. She threw plates. She did him with a pan. Some nights she gave him a dig as soon as she saw him. He never lifted a hand to her. Or to her kids. She gave him language. He swallowed it. He was forever on the move, Jack. He put hisself about. Cased up with the city. Or, as it happens, a night or two with some slag he'd been on the piss with. A bint who worked down the barber's. Get hisself straight before he dipped for his key. He was human. A man. Put his hand in his pocket when he had to. Pay to have his dick sucked. Same as any other cunt. Go with toms but he never brought it home with him. Conventional. Straight as arseholes. Nothing out of the way. Front or back, no refinements. No vaseline. Thought the world of his family, if he had to, if they was on top of him. But he preferred the town, the liberties of East London, rain on his neck. Sooty rain through an open window. The wind whispering down his ear'ole in a speeding motor.

Doubling back down Pitfield Street, alongside the waste ground, Tone's guts started to give him gyp. He knew they was right behind him, up his fucking arsehole. The Bubble had the squits. Now their card had been marked, it was on them. Dirty money killing the hang of his jacket. The hunter had become the hunted. So many faces in the driving mirror, shifting shapes and expressions. And all of them his own. Man of a thousand faces. Tone couldn't find hisself, he aged and he withered. He was wax and linen. He was bone. Oil. Animal. He drew back his lips, tried to, showed his teeth. Blood on them. Jack was still out of it.

Eyes closed, asleep, pretending to sleep, in the mime of it, Jack got this strange feeling about the Bubble. The pills did that. Paranoid ecstatic. He *knew* that the real job, the poxy oncer, the hangman's fee, was for a vanishing act. Him and the Bubble, one or the other, don't matter. One goes and the other is sorted, cops for it. A vacancy. Mated in the act of it, the butchering. One living to tell the dead man's story. A ventriloquist, mouth stuffed with clay and gravel. Look at the cunt behind the wheel. The Bubble was screwing him. There was no fucking Norton. Not Ron. Norton was another name for nothing. An alias. A *nom de guerre*. His mate Tone was on an earner to put him down. He was going to join the firm. On a promise. Him and his brother, that headcase Chris. Jack was on his tod in a car filled with brothers. They were coming from up west to meet the Twins.

Jack had to hold hisself back. Strangle the fucking Bubble in the motor and he's giving them what they want. Fuck that! He'll shove the crooklock down the wop's throat and hook up his lights. Jack could ride through hell in a fiery chariot. He'd walk away from it. 'Arright, Tone? Fancy a drink, son?'

You couldn't put the frighteners on Jack. Nothing to frighten. He was a dead man. An immortal. Turks, Bubbles, Jocks. Wasting their time. The smell of the grass in the summer meadow should have been in his nostrils, but it wasn't. Pitfield Street was the sharp edge of the world. Jack was undescribed by it. Boundaries warped. The hot stench of things cooking in sacks. Pissed mattresses smoulding by unwatched fires.

Jack went into Sam's place in Murray Grove like he owned the gaff. The swagger of a man so drunk he has to busk it from memory, the way one leg goes in front of the other, the elbow on the bar, the nod to the twilight punters, the ciggy lifted from an open packet. That's how the pros drink, settle theirselves for a session. On the bar next to them, packet of fags, flick lighter on top. Pint always half done, within a good swallow of the finish. 'Thanks, Jack. Just one more.' The mouthy cunts always caught out, caught sucking at an empty pot. 'Same again, fellers?'

Dressed like a scarecrow in a thunderstorm, Jack had style. He had edge. The inviolability of the dead. Salt sweat running in channels from under the brim of his graveyard trilby, an actor in a bad script. Jack was on the shelf, watching hisself, seeing how he did it. The Alice was finished. Windows boarded up. The gaff was for sale. Optimistic sale boards fixed to the side of a ruin. Dust and rat droppings. A memory hutch. A bell jar of ferns and spectral voices. Jack was a ghost in an Alzheimer's cardigan. One of those numbers with a fold-over collar. Tone trailed him, nodding grimly to the faces, shooting his cuffs. The saddest living thing on the manor. Terrified that the narrative thread was about to be cut, that he'd lose it. Mute, hearing the same track for ever, the rest of his days. *Knockin' on Heaven's Door*. Jack was Tone's guide, his author. The Bubble had no other purpose. A car wash jockey. A haircut taking his whack out of a defunct coldstore. He torched warehouses while Solly and his mates, bibs and braces, were scoffing the premiums in Bloom's. He was stiff. He didn't have the backbone for treachery. 'Get them in,' Jack said, 'then check the motor.'

Sam's place had gone, no question. But Jack don't see it. There's a little mob, six- or seven-handed, over in the corner. Limehouse Willie, Electric Les, and the rest of the Kray furniture. Talking chairs the lot of 'em. On the blower as soon as Jack makes his entrance. ''Allo Jack mate. Tone. You lost, son?' The usual patter, eyes like flint. Hoodlum priests in uniform black. Initiates of harm. Good company. Small round table top covered in bottles, beer mats, smoking ashtrays. Traders without a trade. Rabbit merchants. Bent talk. Watch the fists knot.

The Bubble sends Sam over with a tray, but he don't leave the bar. He protects his space. He watches the door. There's two entrances, two sides to this. Which accounts for Sam's popularity. The fact that nobody could find this gaff twice. Motors, ready for the off, hidden behind mounds of black bags. Too flash for bandit country, a waste of public housing, dump bins.

Vodka cola, rum and pep, Russian stout, screwdriver, Irish, gin fizz, any name in the book, any port in a storm. No Euro sceptics here. Tray after tray. Anything except lager. Baths of it. Cellars of swill. Your choice. They won't let Jack go. One of the comedians demands Buck's Fizz. They send the bird out for fucking orange juice. Jack matches the lot of them, the pensioners of crime. They love each other to death. A pint for the potman, the sweeper, the idiot. Tanking it, Jack and his afternoon chums. The ones who will feed his pieces to the pigs, stomp him down into an industrial meat grinder, who will render his residue as boneless gristle. Mates. All pissed together.

It turns in an instant. Something on the jukebox. Jack the life and soul, gives it a kick. *No more yoga of the night club.* Bollocks! The heavies won't wear it. But it takes Jack's fancy. Again and again, he has Sam bung in the silver. Each time the first. The song's in Jack's head. *No more yoga of the night club.* (Tone hangs on the other line: 'No one told me the Holy Spirit was a woman.' What the fuck does *that* mean?)

'Turn it in, Jack, for fuck's sake.' One of the faces says the kid who sings it is a poxy minicab driver from Bethnal Green. 'Straight up, run me out the

Isle of Grain for a pony. Lovely feller.' 'What fucking singer, cunt?' There's no singer for Jack, the words are swimming in his head. He knows it's on him. He has his hand down his coat, makes like he's got a shooter. 'Piss off back to those poofs, tell them what I fucking said. Jack is immortal.'

The nutter has the whole mob lined up against the flock. He'd have done them if Tone hadn't stopped him. 'Not here, Jack. Use your head.' They don't need telling, they're out of the door, leaving the wreck of glasses on the table. Jack's shot the colonel's wad, he's potless. They got to lose theirselves. 'Hit the box and have it out of here.' Tone's bottled it. He'll feel better in the motor, cruising as it gets dark, as the lights come on, and the citizens hide theirselves away in their tidy little hutches. You can stack 'em like egg boxes.

Jack's alone on the street. He's all for giving chase. He wants to nail the scum to a tree. 'Five minutes Tone. Toe to toe. On the cobbles.' He's going to ram them, run 'em off the road. He jumps in the Jag, hoists Tone after him. Unfinished business. He can taste the blood, aspirins crushed in ketchup, a paste of broken glass. He remembers dumping Buller Ward on the steps of the London, his boat in ribbons, seeing him walk away. He knows what Ron's like when the vulture pecks his shoulder. Finish it now. There won't be another chance.

Tone reverses out into the road, going backwards faster than yesterday, when the wheels come off. That bastard Willie has loosened the bolts. The engine's roaring and they've done the suspension. They're skidding to nowhere, the wheels running east ahead of them. Jack is pissing hisself. It's the funniest thing that's happened to him in hours. He goes back into the Alice to celebrate.

The Holy Spirit a woman. It plays on the Bubble's mind. Now there's a bitch's face in the mirror strip. Lipstick on his drawn lips. Eyeshadow. He's quite tasty as it happens. Tone is a bird. He's wearing a kind of blue hood. He'd fancy himself if his bollocks hadn't shrunk to the size of frozen peas. If Jack didn't have an arm around his neck. *No more yoga of the night club.* Jack was trying to sing. 'Remember that slapper, Tone, up Highbury? She had a voice. Like a fucking siren.'

Jack was going. Under the river. White tiles in the headlight beams. All that tonnage of water above him. He can't swim, he floats. What if it's not just the Bubble? What if, inside Jack's white shirt, there nestles a pair of firm alabaster breasts? The urge to stop and look, to touch with his hand, is almost irresistible. Just as crossing water is a kind of death, so travel, in the sealed safety of a motor, is an unsexing, an invitation. You can jump gender, abdicate or assume any sexuality you choose. Eyes shut, drifting. Jack has a woman's soul. The Jag is female. It runs on spirit. Listen to the valves, the pistons, petrol burning in pleasurable agony. Jack is being driven off the edge of the world, down the length and mystery of Sheppey, the Isle of Grain, Medway's ruined military detritus. A choirboy, cheek smooth as blossom, at the wheel. Jack's angel. Jack is the message, not the messenger. Flesh cold as mutton. Sheep grazing harmlessly under the curve of the bridge. Jack waking up dead in a meadow. All the city grassed over. Trees breaking the concrete. Alder, birch, chestnut and oak. Whispers on telephones. Wind in the wire. River the colour of his dead father's greatcoat. Sweating in the kitchen. Skillets and side orders of hash. Sunnyside up. Another half, a chaser in a shot glass. Fire in the blood. Headlights making the eyes of the flock shine red. A bottle of cold clear Russian spirit. Water without the recycled toxins. Yellow rust. Dying of thirst. Eager for the Bubble to piss down his throat. Jack calls the route, through the dark neck to Stoke Newington, anarchists and con artists, kike land. Black hats. Evering Road. March in, down the steps. Front it. Knives and carpets, a jukebox requiem. Yoga this, you tangerine poofs. Twist back on your own corruption.

They say, quite wrongly, he tried to do a header through the window. It was the rush, the expulsion of animus. Hate giving itself up. Event pursuing elegy. The posthumous shatter of glass reassembling itself. Spirit dis-embodied. Language jacking it in.

Plenty of times Jack had the tights over his face. Domestics. The old woman accompanying him across the pavement. Polished stock of a sawn-off shotgun pressing in his lap. Face not his face, too much his own. Deformed into himself, a tribalised nose. Coming up from the junction, Jack pulls a silk stocking over his head. The rasp of denier. *Dernier cri* smearing his hooter, dividing him. Head too big for the hole, fearful of breeching it. Hat on top. What a sight! What a frightener! Down Kingsland High Street, the mouth of the market. Dead now, rubbish trucks sweeping the syrups, the peels, the pulped exotics. Darkies hassling bagels. Jack loved the smell of fresh white bread baking in the quiet night. Oven sweat. The rush of cabbies calling for cream cheese and salmon scrapings.

He made the Bubble pull over, before they crossed the line. Off-limits: Sandringham Road, east towards Amhurst. One of those quiet backwaters. He unbuckled his belt, put an arm around his driver's neck, forced him down. The Bubble was a Mediterranean, a towelhead to all intents and purposes. He'd been away, knew the score. He could fifty-eight his passenger. Swallow him. 'Gobble it, you Greek poof.'

Inside, after the first ten years you die. You can't do it. You don't want to. The tit pictures on the wall are pure decoration. Before that it's complicated. The act itself is easy, but the consequences. You leave yourself behind, leave that place. Never returning in the same shape. Part of you goes back to the other, the punk whose activities you are directing. Imagine. Fantasise. Grey semen slipping down the bristles of your chin. Folk will remember Jack because he was murdered. In the pulse of pleasure. Unable to recall who or what he is. The story.

Tone remembers. The Bubble's hand gripping the resting wheel. All nature calm. Jack has the trousers off him, changed for his own. He has taken a fancy to the slight flaring, the matador cut on the hips. The swirl of grey cloth over brilliantly polished slip-ons, fussy buckles. Tone, in his turn, is stuck with Jack's dire drainpipes, wriggling and kicking to get into them. Jack's hand. 'What's favourite, Tone? In the back, you go over and I give you one? Or shall I have you do a brown eye?' He can feel the Bubble responding to it, the shame. Jack undecided which would be the greater humiliation. The way out. The Bubble's cigarette a thread of smoke, unmoving as a candle flame in a windless room.

'Put your foot down, Tone.' Up on the kerb. Moon bouncing in high windows. Kept the motor beautiful, he did. On his fucking knees hoovering the fluff, emptying the ashtray, arm under the seat, shaking the carpets. A little Greek housewife. Get him a pinny and a mobcap. Lovely. Stoke Newington Road, the old cinema, the mosque, the minimarkets, never looked better.

'When you go case with a bird, Tone,' Jack was saying, 'when you're on the job, do you ever, you think about it, let it go?' Night sticky, dust particles, torn blossom on the screen. 'When you're giving her one, ain't you bothered about slipping yourself, losing out, losing your shape?' Now they're drenched with all the lights and colours of the electric garden. The lilies and lily pads of neon. Fascist fireworks. Reds and greens and yellows. Bile and pus with a fire behind it. Names reversed on the slippery glass. Jack's face painted like a tentshow savage. The Jag joins the carnival. 'I never come, Tone. You know that? Not unless I'm coming back.'

Stepping through toys slung out into the garden. He never had a dog. Need to keep the grass down. Sits, splaylegged, on the boy's tricycle. Tips his hat down over his eyes. Keep the hot light out. Jack could never stay indoors, couldn't sit still unless they strapped him to a chair. At the kitchen table, pulling out the stitches. Bright scissors and the old woman's tweezers. Film reversed. He was putting hisself back together. Half an inch of cat gut and it kept coming, he needed a fisherman's reel to hold it, wind it in. Yards and yards. Stapling the skin to the bone. Or it would fall apart. He couldn't stand up. A pile of bones for the dog he didn't have.

Jack had lost it. Out of his fucking tree. The Bubble didn't know what the fuck he was talking about. Shunt him to the club and piss off back to Haggerston, get clear. A meet with the Mills brothers. Take the brothers to see the Twins. On the firm. A prospect. Get his future straight. Down Evering Road. How many times that evening? A light in the basement, shaded and red. On to the club. The Regency. They haven't eaten all day. A bit of steak, red on the side. A splash of claret. Settle the stomach.

You could smell it on the street, the testosterone. The fear. The welcome of booze asthma, smoke. 'Some bastard's dreaming me,' Jack thought. 'I can't draw breath.' It hits you at the door, the bouncers clocking Tone's slacks. Taking care not to catch Jack's eye. The only hat in the gaff, treats the Regency like a shul. Jack standing in a scarlet letter on the pavement, a neon R. Coming or going? Meat caught between his teeth, waiting for the Bubble to make his move. To catch up with the script. Waiting to shove a shooter down his treacherous throat.

As they arrived, the brothers with him in the motor, the Bubble and his Chrissy, Jack turned. Looked back. Evering Road. Where else? There was another Jag behind them, another threesome. How many does it take to re-enact a story? How many times? How many nights, how often must he tell it, lights in his face, before he gets it straight? How many recordings? How many copies of his mugshot, his famous look, each one stealing another breath from his life? Older and older. Another day above ground, deeper into death.

The Bubble was transformed. Jack looked at him, opened his eyes. The Bubble was made from wet glass. Slow glass. Light came out of him at the wrong speed. Man's blood and hope, and human memory. The Bubble was transparent, he had no substance. The neon R was branded on him in beads of red. 'Like the worst letter of them all,' he thought. 'The Devil's letter K.' He was a glass suit, the sheen of him. Hard, fast silk. Jack saw himself, his own reflection, in the Bubble. That's what he was, literally, an evanescence.

Death poured from the cups. As they slowed, pulled up outside the basement, and Jack reached for the door, geared himself for the party, he knew that he'd never again put his foot on the ground. He couldn't reach it. Some bastard had had it away with the wheels. The Jag was floating like a balloon, a windsock. The streets were moonlight canals. Jack dropped his keys in the water. The Jag, as they saw it, opening the door of Blonde Carol's gaff, had flattened into a disk. It was hovering. That's how it looked through the bubble glass diamond. Through the panel at the top of the door. Like a chalk moon caught in a vice, pulled out of shape by malign gravity. Brought to earth.

Jack tipped over, headfirst, reaching for the keys, to fish them out, and met his own face rushing towards him. The bluegrey townscape across the dawn meadow. The wind under the bridge. The Bubble was gold light, the best spray job in the manor. He was the spit and double of Jack, the Byzantine Jack. The hologram. Jack touched him with his finger and the finger went in, leaving no impression, not breaking the chill of skin. Two Jacks. Two unlucky hands. He let it go then, let it happen.

The griff

Professor Norton lingered on - Weldon Kees

High windows. Keep light out.
Can't trust it.

Headache's killing me.

Egg, eye, granite acorn.
Idiot's alchemy.

He's cut me loose. Without a writer, there's no project.

WANTED: INTERPRETER. UNEDITED CITY.

Name:	Unknown
Current alias:	TURNER Axel.
Date of birth:	Unknown.
Place of birth:	Abandoned motor vehicle (Ford Cortina)
Education:	Redundant.
Height:	Yes.
Diet:	Depends who's buying. Vegetable pulp, Guinness.
Occupation:	Photo journalist, performance artist, psychogeographer.
Influences:	Robert Frank, Alvin Langdon Coburn, Sir Edward Kelley.
Current address:	Heneage St., Whitechapel, E.1.
Current project:	Providing pictorial evidence to support research undertaken by a man named Norton. To gain access to - & photograph - the riverside penthouse apartment of millionaire political fixer, & blockbuster novelist, Lord Kawn.
Likely future status:	Viral ghost.

HENEAGE ST E.1

Heneage. Know where that name comes from?
One of the Elizabethan spy-masters.

What am I supposed to do?
Norton has the entire city on file -
but he's left me with no instructions.
I'm being run by a dead man.

TURNER'S CAMERA HAS A MIND OF ITS OWN. INSTEAD OF REPORTING, IT INVENTS. AN UNRELIABLE INSTRUMENT OF FICTION, CURSED WITH MEMORY.

Panel 1: Close on, Turne
Panel 2: What he 'sees'.
the other long hair) givi
crucifix & lish.
Panel 3: What actually 'i

Light's blood!
The vegetable menstruum!

Photography is
exclusion.
All portraits are
self-portraits.
Got to get out.

More spirit less taste.

REMEMBER
keep going.

OLD STREET

WORLD'S OLDEST COMEDIAN IS DEAD

Break through the barriers.

Norton stresses: the view from Kawn's balcony holds the secret of the river. Money is mystery. A successful photograph & that location is lost to the City forever. Light eats memory.

Lambeth. Lamb of the River.
William Blake & Jeffrey Archer.

Who needs a writer?

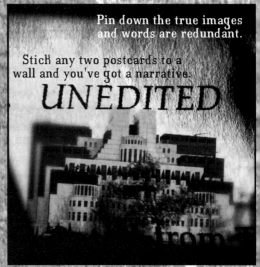

Pin down the true images
and words are redundant.

Stick any two postcards to a
wall and you've got a narrative.

UNEDITED

from

Does Kawn even *write* his own stuff?

Like the rest of us, he takes the
dictation of his controllers. This is a
zone of electromagnetic privilege.
These buildings generate paranoia.
That's their only purpose.

Log the detail. Flesh is stone.

Treat London like an autopsy catalogue.

Get your retaliation in first.

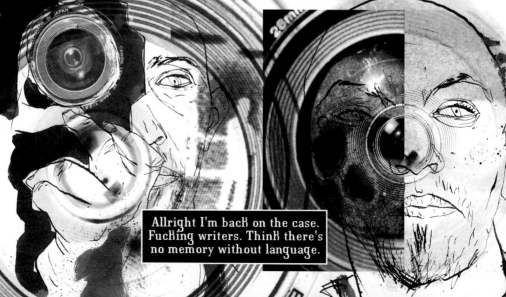

Allright I'm back on the case. Fucking writers. Think there's no memory without language.

Maniac thinks he's in one of Kawn's gash nov...

Tr... climbing after Norton towards penthr...

Th... el. As per page of Kawn typescript. V... etious...

Maniac -
thinks he's in
one of Kawn's
gash novels.

FEAR

~~Feer~~ was unknown to him. Like some ~~agyl~~ ACTILE POWERFUL jungle

creature, he swung, from strut to strut, in

pursuit of his faceless ~~queery~~ QUARRY. Would he be in

time to prevent his enemy from learning the awful

secret of the penthouse? The fact that it was

unoccupied. That no living ~~creeture~~ CREATURE had ever

This gaff needs celebration not investigation

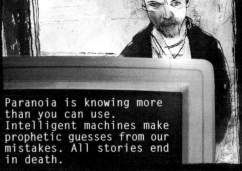

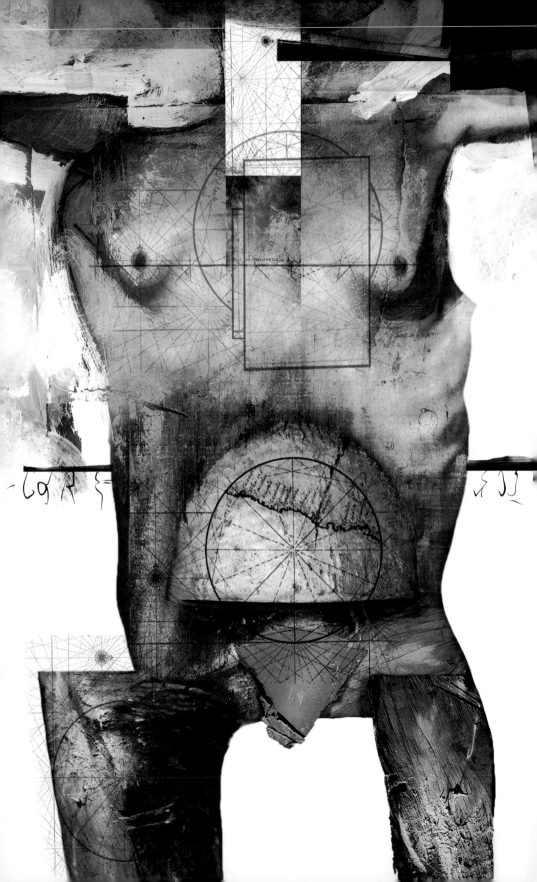

Careful the Horse's Bite

There goes the quintessential Norton.
-Joe Pesci

CAReful the horse's bite

There goes the quintessential Norton

Joe Pesci

This was not what Norton expected. He expected nothing. Didn't know how to expect. Expectation was alien to his temperament. Eyes. He followed. Followed the woman up the stairs. Keeping a safe distance, reminding himself how conversations were launched. The niceties of social intercourse. He muttered to her angular back, made appreciative noises.

And the woman? What could he, without offence, say of her? She was not as he had projected. Projected, yes. A better word. Safe to say that. To admit. Had he formed an image of how a woman, issuing such an invitation, might present herself? How she might look and behave? Well, perhaps. Barely.

'I have a river in my studio which might interest you,' she wrote. And again: 'I would like very much to show you my river.' So he thought of that, the river. Rivers did interest him. But the river and the woman together? Too ripe, too suggestive. The kind of thing that might have to be written about.

Climbing, floor after floor, potted plants at every turn, he began to worry. What river could this be that flowed unmolested under the roof of a converted foundry, out in bandit country, between railway and canal? He'd have no trouble getting his mind around a flooded cellar, a Pythian tributary to the Limehouse Cut. A water theft. A few yards of the Thames subverted. A septic tank masquerading as a holy well. Rivers, connected to the veins, the passage of blood, were easy to visualise. Rivers were an element of any good night's sleep. River women. Rivers with women in them. Birth streams. Slick black depths forced, at crack of day, to release the prisoner sun.

He'd been tricked before. Artists were always dragging him in to see their rivers, which turned out, mysteriously, that very day, to have vanished. Otherwise engaged. Norton was known as a river man. Other writers went for booze, boys, cocaine, Shelley manuscripts, lost novels by Gerald Kersh, a good seeing-to in the back room – but Norton could never resist the chance of plotting a new section of the river. Any river. He fell, time after time, for the notion that certain reaches had been hijacked, spirited away from the tidal stream, made prisoner in Crouch End or Earlsfield. Floods petted and tamed, forced to give up a missing chapter of the great story. There were voices in water. And Norton, watching this woman, had the instinct that she might be one of those who successfully tapped them.

No face. He couldn't see her face. And when he did catch it, as she turned to beckon him, hurry him on, the focus wouldn't hold. It was a sharp face, reckless with intelligence. Sure of itself. Wracked with self-doubt. So that, fearful, he withdrew, replacing the skewed mask with something tamer. An invention. A memory prompt: high cheek bones, slanted eyes, hot shiny skin. A face that came and went before Norton could fix it. It was as if the woman on the stairs noticed this subtle treachery, this comparison of herself with another. She torched Norton to cinder. Then her confidence went. That he might be the one with the courage to see her river.

Now they were passing an anthology of doors. She didn't know which one to pick, which slab of wood was particular to Norton. Words the woman had sent him, a vanity booklet she had published, came back as she fiddled ineffectually with the lock. 'Friends. Pursuers. Some few men.' With her connections, she'd probably gone for lower case and no punctuation. He translated her words into prose. What, he wondered, had happened to those 'few men'?

Norton had no understanding of his own sexuality, except how to control it. And he wasn't very good at that. Did he have a sexuality any-more? Had he ever had a sexuality? Of the vernacular kind? A functioning pump? Signal, response, chemical trigger? (What had sexuality to do with this visit? There was some connection, in Norton's mind, with the unlock-ing of doors. That moment of fumbling with keys, dipping into handbag or raincoat pocket. Some incident on a dingy landing, recalled or imagined.)

Who was this woman? Soon it would be too late. The door was closing. He would be inside. He spun around. There was no door. It had fitted seamlessly back into the white wall of a large bare room. Was she a lycanthrope? He stared at the mouth, the hands. No trace of fur. About his own age. Surely not? Swift, nervous eyes magnified by severe spectacles. She sat and waited. For him. It was his turn. There was no other chair. He paced.

He'd located the foundry with no difficulty, curious to find the gates open, the surveillance cameras nonchalantly panning the clouds. No blood red moons, no howling wolves. Wrong season. The lull between a summer that didn't arrive and the first rains of autumn. Grey early, now relenting, a lacquered, golden interlude of soft shadows and flashing puddles on the tow path. Norton was in a sentimental mood. At the mercy of his biology. Wanting to spend his affection, abrade a smooth shoulder with his rough chin, inhale body perfume, sweetness. Come back to life. Food. Talk. Giving and receiving. The exchange of confidential fluids, mammal identities.

It pricked him, the anticipation, as he made the short journey from Tower Hamlets Cemetery where he'd kipped. Sour coffee to soften the bagels on Burdett Road. Animals caged in pet shops, pissing their fear. A black-glassed massage parlour to relieve the tense knots of diesel-traffic.

Garages in the lee of the railway embankment. Entropy enclosures: breaking-down, repairing, patching together. Machine narratives. The creation of new aliases.

Plenty of so-called artists, in the old days, had gone to ground in this neck of the woods. River pilots who had lost their licences. Visionaries who thought it 'fun' to fail, postponing the possibility of Mount Fuji to a more propitious occasion. Always another horizon to attempt, another disaster to celebrate. Half these characters had decided to make that 'neck of the woods' metaphor literal, to suspend themselves from the lower branches of the boneyard forest. Feet kicking, as they swung, a frantic pattern in the dirt. The dance chart of a suicide tango. No better place to ship out. Roots that thrived on the bounteous dead. Ivy to devour all inscriptions. Rook tribunals. Birds to peck clean the gaping sockets. Stone ships going down, again and again on storm-tossed memorials.

This was worse. A harsher assignment. It was a miracle that her notes had reached him, never sleeping, if he could help it, under the same roof twice. She'd persuaded him into a studio where there was no trace of a river. A more riverless billet he had never encountered. His thirst was terrible. A stone-sucking, tongue-blistering drought that made speech impossible. She relented and passed him a small plastic bottle of mineral water.

He was impressed, he had to admit, by the quality of her silence. He searched, vainly, for a window. The confirmation that the railway, the stubby estates, the deserted afternoon roads, were still out there. He strained for the martial rumour of an ice-cream van.

The woman was calling the shots. She was the one with the fire, Why had she chosen *him*? There had obviously been others, the men alluded to in her pamphlet. They had failed and were to be seen no more. Pursuers pursued. Professional voyeurs, culture-drones with effortlessly formed opinions, put to the test. Norton felt, for the first time, like Walt Whitman, when he received strange, scented correspondence from England. On coloured notepaper. What does she want of me? The shock of receiving an unsolicited letter. Getting word into that one-night dosshouse. He was assured of her determination, her will. The taint of madness. Creativity on the turn. Insufficiently recognised and acknowledged. (There can never be enough recognition. Loud enough praise. Enough sympathy. Genius is not

– ask Peter Pytchley – its own reward.) She was her work's bride, its bachelor. Her child, torn bloodily from the womb, was offered for inspection.

The room, the studio. That's all he had to work with. A smile in her direction could be misconstrued. This fettered intelligence demanded a form. The woman stepped back into the aether and was replaced by a black cat, a jaguar. A sleek fur coat and painted talons. She breathed meat and poppies. She circled his fumbling attempts at language. Then the terrifying spectacles reappeared on the end of her nose. The gloss paint was stripped. She was sensible and panting with the excitement of the game. That he, dumb as stone, should discover her river.

In a moment she would clap her hands like an Edwardian child at a conjuring show. He was initiated into her conspiracy of excellence. She struggled with the neck of the water bottle. Her movements were almost spastic. Time and obscurity had worn her down. Her nervous system was on the point of collapse. A blue flame. A light fault. The intensity of her concentration in this indifferent space. A room as complacent as an odalisque.

He toured. He scoured the walls for a sign. Some dialogue he could steal. A speech bubble. A prompt. He looked, in essence, for something to look at. She had removed everything from the room that might have helped him: no books, no clock, no postcards. For an instant, he thought he understood – this was a conceptual gig, the blank room *was* the art. Whatever happened, happened. The room was the presented version of itself. He, in describing it, would grant it life.

He couldn't. He didn't have the qualifications. Didn't have the geometry for it. If she had stood up, done a twirl, given him a bit of chat, he could have attempted a crude sketch. Through grotesque exaggeration, he revealed character. He'd always cheated with buildings. Used the ones that had already been mapped by better men. At a pinch, he could fall back on his photographs. Not now, not today. No camera. No story.

If he had nothing to say, he was here for ever. Unless he could respond to the minimalism of the situation, it would hold him. The narrative would not develop. There would be no plot, no sub-text, no shocking revelation. A woman invites him into her studio. He foolishly accepts. And . . .

And nothing. The woman was disobligingly inert. She refused to transform herself into a wolf. She offered no exotic cordial. She had no riddle to ask. She was not a long-lost sister, a spurned mistress in disguise. She was not, not even that, an avatar of Norton. Norton in drag. His feminine self. His anima. Not an owl or a gyr falcon. Not a bitch, a dominatrix, an angel of death. The jaded hack tried them all. No go. Not a trick that any sane editor would accept for publication. Nothing that could be rewritten, punched up, revised, atomised into a comic strip.

She smiled. 'There's no way in,' she said. The river was pinned to the far wall. Now he saw it, a scroll. The shape of a cat, poised to spring. A drawing, a print. An unembarrassed art work. A manifestation. Thank god! He lurched towards it. Fast black lines, contour marks, cancelled or inadequately inked. Iron filings disturbed by a magnetic field. Migrating swallows. A rush of energy-blisters that described a gentle meander. Not quite the Thames, but not entirely a stranger to it. Call it a river if you will. And she had. This was what she wanted him to see.

No, it wasn't. What she wanted to see was his reaction to the humped shape: so sophisticated in its apparent naïvety. Black and white wave-crests scudding across thick paper. The scroll could be read in either direction. It would be rolled up and removed. But that would not cancel or reverse the direction of the river. He had to speak, or drown in the silence. He turned his face away from her.

He was mute. So was she: chaffing, snorting, provoking. The scroll grew louder. Norton saw the river, the surrogate. Saw it in its essential riverness. More of a river than the Thames. Which remained local, visible, over-described. Heavy, wet, stinking, at the mercy of wind and tide.

The scroll, Norton decided, was a chart. Of the kind that could be purchased from Kelvin Hughes' basement at 145 Minories. Impractical but aesthetically pleasing. A chart for landlubbers. Numbers, depths, sandbars, marine obstacles. (The skippers Norton knew put to sea with a couple of pages of an outdated A–Z, that could, in an emergency, be used for a roll-up.) The elegant fiction of documented fact. Too much reliance on this object, returned to its weatherproof, cellophane pouch, would leave you up to the oxters in black mud.

The river in the studio was made of words. He had to cruise them, test the current. Get the ink against his nose. 'Arcades . . . Across the sanded floor of the café . . . The courtyard . . . of the torchbearer.' Each section a repetition, a variation on the last. Any few yards of river, if framed in a glass box, would look the same. But the same words, broken sentences, when they are repeated, are *not* the same. The displacement alters. Norton understood that he was not supposed to stand here reading the scroll. But the thought came to him, the horror, that he might once have written it. This liquid, provisional book. His own words – or words he had stolen – cast into another, unpredictable form. Was he proposing a journey already made? Or casting a future excursion? Avoid, at all costs, that dubious word, 'arcades'. Foreign. Surreal. Decadent. Forcing the mouth into a carp-like yawn.

'You know that I stalked you?' said the woman. With dry-lipped relish. 'At your heels all the way down Lea Bridge Road and you never suspected. From the portico of the Orphan Asylum to the terrace of the Alfred Hitchcock. When you took a photograph, I entered it in my notebook. When you scribbled, I caught you on film.'

She was hysterically bright now. 'Body exhausted of its nervous force.' Confident of his attention. There was more river than he knew what to do with. The black ink elements glistened in snakeskin. He remembered (invented) shoes with that pattern. Violet tights distressed along the same lattice. A woman in another room, at this hour of the day. Yawning, opening the shutters. Watching a fat man lumber along the harbour wall, doubled against the wind. Small craft tossing at anchor in the sheltered bay. And later, when he was alone, the long, steely sunset.

In the windowless room the scroll with its swift black lines was the only source of illumination. She was giving him nothing. The scroll was a body-wrapping, unwrapped. A heat print. A score. He couldn't resolve it.

'I passed you a card then. In the café. Now it's your turn. Tell me what you think.'

This was no easier, but he was getting used to it. Some of the words shone. In the way that a bead of accidental spit gleams like a jewel on the screen of a word processor. He was ready to put the questions. Almost ready. If she was still there in the darkening studio, hugging herself, knees clutched under her chin.

The river was his way out. The river was made of damaged texts, printed again and again, one on top of the other, until they became abstractions.

These were not his words, not yet. They would only be his if he transcribed them. If he chose to edit them into an exit line, a conclusion. He could contrive a report, more or less true, and send it to McKean. Let the illustrator visualise the scene, process it in his oast house. His state-of-the-art studio. Feed it to his Japanese fish. In the safety of McKean's world text could become image, words would be isolated, photographs warped and set over fabulous maps. The non-river could be unimagined. A river of words. Let McKean fix it in an allotted number of pages. Nothing of the woman remained. A pair of spectacles. A lock of hair. The shape of a jaguar pressed against a scroll. Something growling at the undiscovered door.

ii

The second woman, years before this, also invited Norton to look at what she had made. She was younger. Younger then than the river woman was now. Norton had been fucking her, fiercely, tenderly, both laughing, against a wall. No. He had noticed her, perhaps that was it, the more probable version, with another man, a Rasta, as he walked, at the wrong time of day, towards Fashion Street. (And again, behind Kings Cross, talking to a man in a car.) She was too driven, too compulsive, to be an artist. Better than that. Lacking the cold eye, the detachment. But she made art, dragged it out of what she knew. Judged her life by how it came, the discoveries, spasms, seizures. How it felt, rather than how it looked. How well the objects might represent themselves in another person's fantasy.

They'd had a meal, had they, in a formica-table Bengali slop-joint? No white punters. No booze. Cold water from a tin jug. Painted tigers and an emerald lake. No sawdust, no prospect of arcades. She suffered from a slight cold. Flushed. Her leather jacket slung over the back of her chair. The pub before that. The room with the pool table, away from the strippers. She smoked. Took make-up well. Dressed down for the occasion. Work jeans, boots. A risk-taker with the time to construct a proper face. High cheekbones. Slanted Slavic eyes. Something pouty, milk-rich, chipmunk, about her. Not unpleasant. Good talker. (If Norton hadn't been a party to this conversation, then he was in the restaurant, at another table, making notes. The back of his head in the mirror. The girl's eyes watching him watch her.)

This was a different tale. She'd found him. Found her way to where he was. In the market caff at breakfast time, lingering over a second mug of coffee, deciding on that day's walk.

In she strides, the confidence of money somewhere down the line. Nocturnal face, vivid. Straight up to him, as if she recognises what he's for. Seeks him out. As if he had some part of a story that she needed. He feeds her. Puts the questions. Lets it unfold. No studio, thank God for that. Her work seems to involve the streets, archaeological retrievals, memory games. The entire district is her studio. She discovers resonant spaces. Discovers him. Solicits language. She's retrieving a narrative from these fragments. Herself a work of art, a character stepping out of the text, to ensure that her story is properly told. Hair swishing over the nape of her black polo-neck sweater. Urgent. 'The courtyard . . . under the Arcades . . . the torchbearer.'

A great girl. Norton is fond of her already. She doesn't want him to explain her to herself. She is not looking for appreciation. The perfect audience. He hopes there is nothing for him to see, to handle. He loves her mania, the way she has given herself to this quarter of the city. The furious tilt of her eyes.

If they'd stayed in the caff, there would have been no problem. He was safe with postcards. The way she had turned into paste rectangles all the objects found in the dead man's basement. (Any river, there, would be a river of blood.) She has photographed every item the investigators found when they broke in. The bunch of keys. The hairbrush. The collarless shirt. The fur in the kettle. The hermit's film-fan postcards. She has made postcards out of postcards.

And it was all fine with Norton. He could live with that. They walked away together. There was no question, then, of physical conjunction. Although, full-bellied, salt teasing the tongue, it was on his mind. One of those friendly, conversational morning fucks. She led him, before he bothered to think about where he was, down some steps. Into the ullage cellars of the old brewery. The stores' cupboard where the mythical caretaker had hidden out for so many years, after the brewery had been asset-stripped and allowed to drift into a business-art limbo.

There was even, he noticed, a heavy rubber torch in his hand. He panned the dusty shelves of tools and boxes, mouse-droppings, chains, labels weathered to insect husks. Ink the colour of rust. Beneath the mumbling pipes, beneath the cold flags. Beneath the stables. She is like the new proprietor. The vanished caretaker with his tablets of angel magick, his arcane dictionaries. Spider-fur, paper-skin spread tight between her fingers. Perfume of body warmth. Benylin. Night dancer. Clubber. Smoke caught in carded wool.

Norton has been invited, under the ground, to curate the dead man's relics. To mythologise them. But can he revise what has not yet happened? This is not a suitable subject. Too predatory, too much involved with the fever of the girl's lips, moving, whispering, isolated in the white beam of the torch. Her sharp teeth.

The river is the spill of cards on the café table. Picture masking picture. Random collages of cancelled objects. She sits back. There it is. She will travel, move out. Ullage slops rush between Norton's feet. The river in the basement. Rumours of blind dogs, rats, subterranean pig packs diverted from the Fleet. That is the challenge: to go back, to become the caretaker. To double for him. Without hope of reward or escape. Without text. In the darkness of the failing battery. Unscripted. Dispossessed.

The only photograph, discovered years later in a secret drawer of the cupboard, is one that somebody else has taken. The girl sitting on a table. In this room. Books. A sewing-machine. Tins. A single, flaring lightbulb. This room as it is yet to become. As it was photographed by another man. The lurching skinhead Norton saw, now it comes into focus, striding into a courtyard, his arm around the girl's waist. The shocking intimacy of their embrace.

iii

*U*neasy. Not climbing. No stairs, not this time. No descent into a picaresque basement. Ordinary. As you'd expect. Institutional. More like an industrial estate than a nest of artists' studios. The sort of place you'd finish up in, checking and rechecking your map, if you were searching for an obscure magazine distributor or a firm that repaired car radios.

Norton wandered through blocks of similar, low level, wire-mesh windows, stopping from time to time to read the message on his card, the address and the number. He hadn't taken the message himself. The girl in the pub answered the phone. But the call was definitely for him. He had to go at once to Clerkenwell. A street that he didn't know. The woman, young woman, would be waiting for him there. She didn't wink, the barmaid, but gave him what could be described as an old-fashioned look.

This was his last artist. Because nothing had been resolved by the previous encounters, the plot carried just enough undisclosed content for one final shot. Visiting studios: an essay in three parts. An invitation from a woman he didn't know. A part of the town that was unfamiliar, or insufficiently explored. A small mystery. These women were never the same. They couldn't have been more different. In approach, attitude, appearance. The harnessing of them together was all Norton's doing. Author as editor.

The woman in the third encounter was always the most exciting. Faceless. Nothing but the sound of a human voice. The reported sound. So that she borrowed some of her colouring from the barmaid, whose red hair took the afternoon light in a peculiarly affecting way. A dust of freckles on the shoulder. Norton was, forgive him if you can, an unredeemed romantic.

The door opened to the sound of his voice, to his request. They had him on tape as he walked into the building. Strip-lighting fizzed in its tubes. The kind that made any subtleties of shading or cross-hatching impossible. Battery farm cubicles of the least exalted kind. No names on the doors. He'd had enough of these supplicants. Let him find his own fictions. Nothing left. His reflexes were dull, spongy. Thomas Burke, a writer he'd known well, but seen infrequently, warned him about this. 'No man who isn't born in London can ever grasp the essence of the city. Not Stevenson, nor Machen. Not Dickens. They remain outsiders, provincials, no matter how many facts and petty histories they manage to absorb. Give it up now, before it's too late.'

Strange cove, Burke. Face of a fourteen-year-old schoolboy. A wanderer who shared Norton's conviction that you should never go back, never revisit old neighbourhoods, schools, lodging-houses, places of employment. That's what fiction was for, to write them out. Erase them. Tommy had tipped him the wink, back in '32, *City of Encounters*. The skull-suckers who would try to tempt him inside, off the street, away from movement. Break the arc of a journey. Infiltrate his narrative. Maniacs, pseudo artists, with their collections, boxes of nuts and bolts scavenged from the gutters. Rabids who spent long nights unscrewing public notices. Stalkers and serial gatherers of tram tickets. Bookmen who did not read. Autograph hunters who could not write. Laundry raiders. Shoe sniffers. A stammering kid who insists on buying you a can of Bengali cola. A man who records the sound of the tide under the pier at Tilbury. But who will not play it back to you. The weirdest of all was the wild-eyed suit who burst into the room where Norton was sleeping and demanded to be allowed to watch him. Ten minutes would suffice. Awake or snoring like a drain, it didn't matter.

Tommy knew them all. He was one of us, eliminated from all the directories. Without recognition or status. Characters he invented would accost him every time he set foot outside his door. That's why he kept moving. That's why he never returned to a district he had previously sampled. Should he offer his hospitality to a mythologised girl, the fiction would overpower him. Become an obsession. And then the girl would vanish. Implicating him in a crime that had never happened.

Norton blundered through the building, imagining the woman who would be waiting for him. No surprises left. No capacity for appreciating new forms of art or expression. He was bored with metaphors. Glutted with brilliance. He couldn't remember – and he was grateful for it – a more tedious setting. No reprise of the Spitalfields basement. No close encounter with an archivist of impermanence. Hutch after hutch of conceptual doodles. Word processors on Ikea tables. Unwashed coffee mugs. An absence of newspapers. The Clerkenwell studio-block was deserted, out-of-season. Nothing worthwhile ever came of a ground-floor expedition. The great tales were all skulking in attics, simmering beneath floorboards.

Where was the bitch? He followed the bullet holes, the trail of empty bottles, into the heart of the clapboard labyrinth. Private spaces partitioned out of an echoing redundancy. Battery cages for the production of singularities. Brood cells. Cubicles lit by a blue interference of welding guns.

After the necessary expenditure of time, the frustration, the ennui, the anger, he found her. Found it. The third woman's studio. Except that it wasn't. It was borrowed space. Some man had the use of it. Foul cigar stubs, greasy notebooks. Phone numbers and quotations from the *Tibetan Book of the Dead* disfigured the white walls. Socks hanging from the drawers of a gunmetal filing-cabinet. Broken weaponry bandaged in wet plaster. Foil takeaway dishes used as ashtrays.

But the woman was present. More so than her host, who, in the great tradition, used his studio as a *pied-à-terre*, a convenience, somewhere to change for dinner. His art was conversation, field sports, the planning of river trips. This was a sponsored dormitory for those nights when he was too drunk to find his way upstairs.

In the corridor, honing in on the scent of kummel, L'*Air du Temps*, cordite, vindaloo, Toscani, Norton flashed to the artist, the woman. Revealed as a sleek-winged bird. Isis. Naked. Light-spliced. A bride of the crystal. Death dancer. Yellow paper fantasies. She was nothing like that. Much more dangerous.

The studio was empty, apart from her patron's trash. Postcards of the man in performance, face squashed like tyretracks on a Chelsea bun. Nothing. No trace. Another fraud. Another wasted afternoon. Nothing but a familiar scroll. It had found him again. He'd made nothing of it the first time. The river of words. The fragmented story. 'This was not what Norton expected.' Overprinted. The same jagged pulse marks. The same tidal ripples. Norton, alone in the studio, unobserved, could begin to read the text. Take it at his own pace.

The river shifted down through the building, from the garret under the eaves to the broom-cupboard in the cellar. The river was not important. It contained the first artist's spectacles as well as a leather jacket, the torn pages of a schoolboy diary. This was a fascinating development. Norton moved in.

The scroll took up the entire space of the studio's dividing wall. It *was* the wall: tier after tier, street after street, a town mapped and discriminated. Inside the drawing – red or brown chalk – there was movement. Arcades in which the viewer could stroll. The effect was vertiginous.

But just at the point where the concept was overwhelming, and the alternate city was about to tumble, engulfing the seduced spectator, he found himself sucked inwards. The composition was indistinguishable from his perception of it.

Torch in hand, he could float over the sanded floors of deserted cafés. He could read a menu from the wrong side. There were no people, that was a bonus. No colours other than earthy reds. The woman who had drawn this world had genius; flowing, unbroken inspiration coupled with an autistic steadiness of eye. Her world-city was a theatre. It was divided into galleries, walkways. Cloisters. There was no escaping them. A night city that a single traveller is privileged to explore. A city of the blind, with no shadows, no shading. No hooded figures in deep recesses. No trade. A city of the enlightened dead. A city beneath the sea.

Norton's footprints, as he trod on the powdery paper, became part of an infinitely complex pattern. If he knew how to navigate he could travel anywhere in time. He could escape. If he knew how to use a crayon, if he had the gift for it, he could design an exit. A gap in the trees. He could construct a boat. Norton, out on the waves, in an egg-box ark. Norton with a beard like Noah.

This was an unlooked for exhilaration. The woman, the artist, was with him in her fantastic city. The others had been her messengers, shaping initiations, toying with the quest hero. Norton lost his vigilance. He was ready, should he find one, to risk a mirror. He was owl-faced, feathered. He was anything that took her fancy. Adrift in a city that altered as his under-standing of it altered. That grew, developed, branched out in fractal abundance.

But he was still a pedant, still obliged to work his way gingerly down through the composition, level by level, line by line, from the top lefthand corner. He was dizzy. The shock of being inside the thing he had been looking at. Twisting to see over the edge of the balcony. Breathless at the plunge of it. Seeing down to what lay in the theatre's pit. No air to swallow. Clammy. The inside of the outside. The chalk trap. Crayon veins opened. No depth. No back to the paper. Norton's error: to impose himself on the composition. Not to be satisfied with undirected consciousness. The desire to control, make sense, find drama in abstraction.

The voices, far away, of the artist and her patron, in the studio, debating their arrangements, not discussing this. Where Norton is. No city of the imagination. No theatre of blood. No public playhouse for private drama. The galleries and tunnels and ladders and ropes are bone and wood. Movement is the movement of Norton's breath on a white sheet. As they open him, fillet him like a herring on an aluminium dish. Hacksaw his rib-cage. A smoking drill. As they stitch the chambers of his heart with platinum threads. And do not let him die. As they draw the crow out of his peeled scalp. As they mark him with felt-tip pens. Gross lines become the verticals of the woman's monstrous composition. A drawing that is the world. A star field coaxed down into a thatched oval.

Norton falling from his balcony, covers his eyes. The eyes of the corpse on the table. That all this light, these high conceits – the detail – have escaped from an autopsy sketch. A woman who has the permission of the morgue. The freedom to come and go amongst the confused dead. A visionary technician. A person skilled in the unfolding of post-human possibilities. A slow autopsy turning the frozen air to chocolate. The chalk line to a muddy brown. To a river.

In living his death, in the foreknowledge gifted to him by this remarkable art work, Norton absorbs, is absorbed by, his conceptual woman. The wall, and the scroll on the wall, is the map of his fear. The chart by which Burwell will plot his course towards the off-shore falcon towers. The city of encounters. Twice warned, twice willing. Now a hand, which is faster, surer than his own, lifts out his hammering heart.

He can look in a scintilla of ghost light at the upper gallery. The face of the woman, blank eye, gazing over her lover's shoulder in the Whitechapel yard. At something that pretends to be his soul. A black mess of worms and feathers. He becomes what he is unable to describe.

# of The viii Falconer

I mean what sort of man is it that writes down his
own dreams? And then tells you - Tim Binding

at 5.38am. on the morning of the 3rd. of august, Horus in the ascendant, Peter Pytchley, author, falcon-breeder, savant, died of a massive, sunburst coronary. He was alone in his Battersea flat and attempting to crawl towards the telephone. at that instant his spiritual twin, his fetch, broke free. Now able to pursue his own dark agenda. To assume another identity: **as pure fiction**.

xeperu   em   bak

the transformation   into   a hawk

4. Extreme high angle. Ambulance crossing Battersea Bridge.

Voice: "Frankie, phone. Some hospital."

of hi-tech hospital on Fulham Road.
(Based on St Stephen's Hospital
Hospital as luxury hotel/airport.

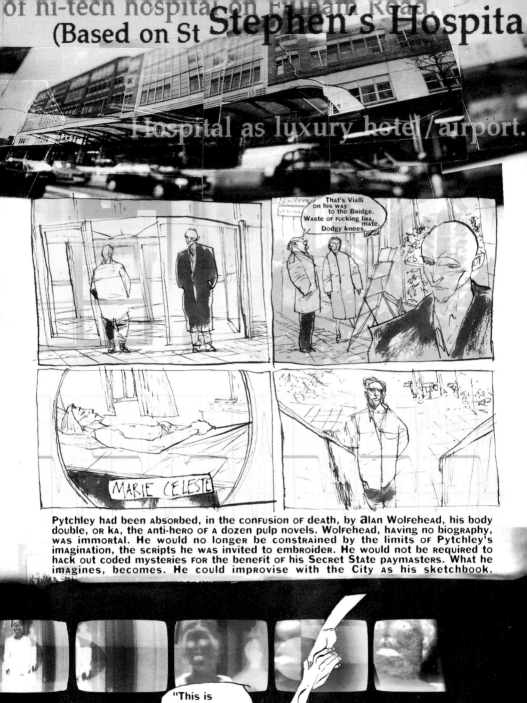

Pytchley had been absorbed, in the confusion of death, by alan Wolfehead, his body double, or ka, the anti-hero of a dozen pulp novels. Wolfehead, having no biography, was immortal. He would no longer be constrained by the limits of Pytchley's imagination, the scripts he was invited to embroider. He would not be required to hack out coded mysteries for the benefit of his Secret State paymasters. What he imagines, becomes. He could improvise with the City as his sketchbook.

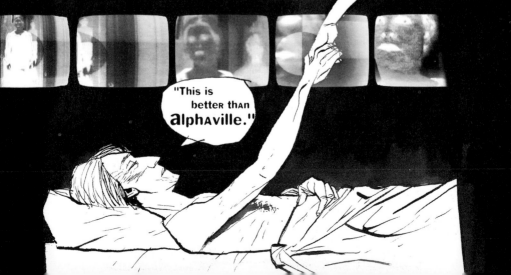

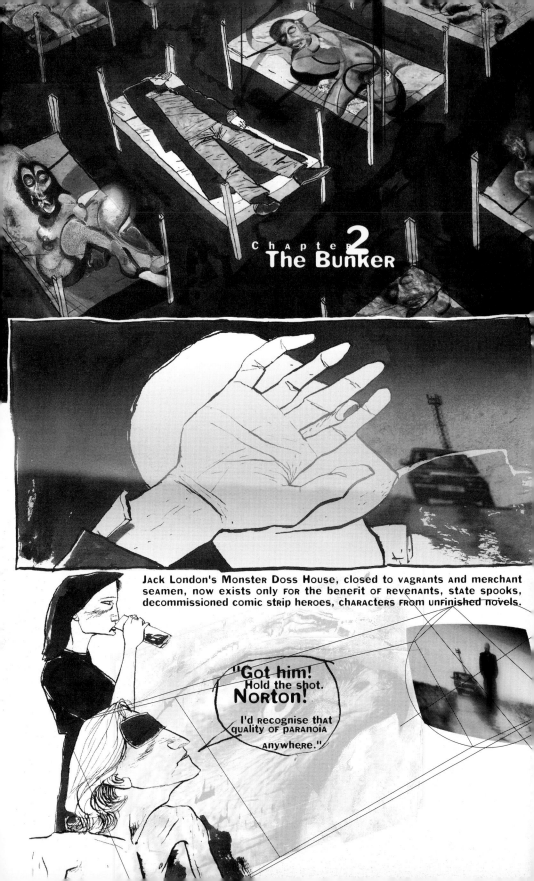

Chapter 2
The Bunker

Jack London's Monster Doss House, closed to vagrants and merchant seamen, now exists only for the benefit of revenants, state spooks, decommissioned comic strip heroes, characters from unfinished novels.

"Got him!
Hold the shot.
Norton!

I'd recognise that quality of paranoia

anywhere."

3. Sequence of consecutive images

small panels,

SIMPLIFIED SECTIONAL DRAWING OF THE BUNKER AT KELVEDON HATCH

Norton walks over brow towards fake Essex farmhouse.

This is, in fact, the Kelvedon Hatch Secret Bunker.

Norton up steps and into building. (The fake farmhouse conceals a bunker with three levels. See diagram.) He walks through steel doors and down long tunnel.

Olga pushing Wolfehead in wheelchair, up hospital.

Away from us.

Recorded voice (in bunker, from concealed speakers): "Condition red! North Weald, Biggin Hill, West Malling. Down. Utter devastation. City destroyed. River ablaze. Seal all doors. Guards to the perimeter fence."

"Concentrate, he's slipping you."

"I can't..."

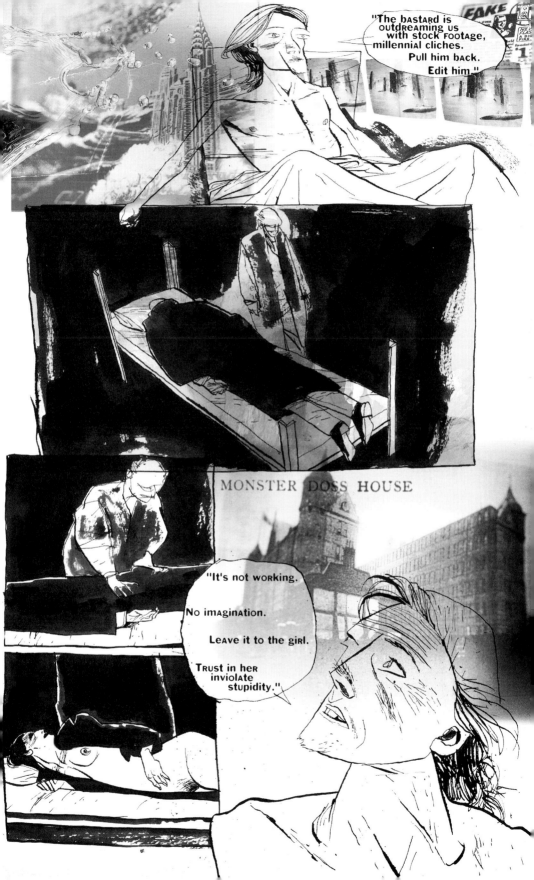

Chapter 3
The National Portrait Gallery

TWO GENTLE M EN

Alex could find a vein in a mummy.

OF S ix O H O

William S. Burroughs

two gentlemen OF soho

Alex could find a vein in a mummy
William S. Burroughs

*C*oming too quickly away from ... Surfeited, thick-headed with redundant imagery, he plunged into a confusion of narrow streets and courts. The perfume of the crowd, the art mob, irritated his nostrils. Snatches of conversation playing back, drove him deeper, faster, into the labyrinth. Words, if he did not burn them, would revive the physical sensations of those hysterical rooms. Liverish portraits in satellite galleries. Candyfloss flesh. A misapplied notion of immortality. Better to piss your outline in acid on a red, sandstone wall. Better trash your life, your aspirations in a rack of airport yellowbacks. Writing fiction was the best guarantee of anonymity. Nobody, thank God, wanted to know what Norton looked like. Better sell your daughter to a garlic pharaoh, watch her ravishment, than tolerate this wine-swilling bonhomie. This grotesque adulation of the artist. Norton was dedicated to invalidating the past, hacking the turf from beneath his feet, never paddling down the same sewer twice.

The streets were unknown, over-familiar. They took too much on themselves, replete with bad script, excess narrative. They nudged Norton towards episodes of which he had no memory. The stones remembered *him*. They bid him welcome. They whispered. They planted pictures in his mind, anticipated his travels. They would have him stop and stare at faces displayed outside peephole clubs, at cellophane magazines, innocent of text.

Each viewer, each visitor to the Axel Turner exhibition, however pre-occupied, would work some revision into a favoured portrait that caught the eye. They would polish a button, lace a shoe. Correct a crooked smile. See what they wanted to see in a mess of dark shapes. Those large photographs in their black frames were blots, inky obstructions, affected by the observer's failure of nerve. The art buffs wanted more, much more, than the portraits could give them. They wanted movement. Life. They wanted frames to turn into doors, to let them through. They wanted, by successfully interpreting these patterns from the past, to gain access to that fabulous kingdom. To be there. They wanted to know what would happen next. What was said in the instant before the photographer clicked his shutter.

Turner's prints were prophetic, unsubtle winks at posterity. Shame-lessly importuning anybody stupid enough to pay them some attention. 'Use me,' they bleated. 'Take me.' Blink in their direction and they'll lift their skirts. They need your collaboration. They need a host-body prepared to soak up used light. Norton was too weary, too out of kilter with himself, to oblige. He'd lost control of his consciousness. His walk, as ever, was an attempt at unravelling the choke of imagery; disposing of it in exercise, exhausting himself to the point where sleep would be as black as a dead ocean. Every photograph in the show had its own mileage-counter, nudging the viewer towards an appropriate location, a contrary landscape. There was a subtle relation between intensity of vision and distance-to-be-travelled. Three hours on the road, eyes shut, might make amends for a glimpse at the scowling painter pictured in Paddington. A week, barefoot above the snowline, would palliate an inexpert glance at a pair of suicided inverts. One print in particular, though he would not speak of it, fed upon him, as he was sustained by its slow decay.

This is why he scuttled. This was the source of his panic: that Norton himself should be caught on film! Shot as he watched, a face in the crowd. Exposed at last to another writer's interpretation.

He had in his pocket a talisman, a postcard. The mechanical process of producing the object, glossing the thick card, neutralised its venom. It was a photograph of the photographer, the thing that may not be captured. Why will those deluded creatures not understand the bargain they make, the signature in blood and alcohol? They are a caste apart. Corpse handlers. They should wear a glass eye on a chain around their necks. Make payment for what they do. It is false magic, all of it. That is its strength. That is why those who have never been photographed, when they finally succumb, have such a charge. Why virgin prints sing with radiant light.

Here was the man celebrated by posthumous exhibition. A man re-vealed. But there was no stamped credit, an image without proper attribu-tion. A canny snapshot. Self-portraits by photographers are tautologous, an obscenity. It can't be done. The posturing, the making ready, and the heat-theft. Cannibalism. The pose is too calculated, too knowing. The snapper struggles to act himself, impersonate an absence. Bad theatre. Stupidity.

Norton's trophy was more obliging. The man, the weasel, caught on a bar stool, by an amateur who had snatched up the abandoned Rolleiflex and turned it on its user. No wonder the photographer lost some part of his equipment every time he went on a shoot. Cameras have to be worked or they sulk. There he was, match in hand: 'You don't know what the fuck you're doing, Frank.' The painter, the one who has usurped his role, is as drunk has he is (not drunk enough). He can't treat the image as he'd want to. Can't smear it. Come back on it the next day. Sweat it until the subject of the portrait, the runt, the mistake, confesses. Gives himself up.

Would it be enough, this postcard in the pocket? External elements were dressing Norton's mood. He tried to push west, twisting, tapping for dust-veins, avoiding the busier tributaries, the white chairs on the pave-ment. Men with their faces pressed against voice boxes in narrow doorways. Third-floor punters. Cutting-room pros with lungs full of image smoke. Fast-hand assistants, women who work. Slow-glass windows with their dark secrets, their posters and promises. Empty film cans. Over-flowing dustbins. Basement sweat-boxes that didn't try too hard to in-veigle an audience. Soft stairs. Bead curtains. Spastic performances better left to an empty room. The girls Norton saw, the gum-chewers, were ghosts. They couldn't remember themselves. But the men behind them were grounded, ballasted with coin. They were who they were, no one else, solid as a night in Northampton.

Norton's technique, if you could call it that – he walked quickly, rarely breaking his stride, unless his game leg dragged against the lip of the curb – was to get through it, this maze of his own contriving, as fast as he could, choosing, always, the least obvious entry, the narrowest, dirtiest lane. He thought he walked quickly, but women went past him, without appearing to hurry or to strain. They seemed to know where they were going, which gave them the advantage. That and their age, the suitability of their dress. They cruised, Norton burrowed. He raged when he found himself seduced into a dead-end, brought up short by a private security barrier. He cursed. Scratched. Picked up speed again. He moved so fast, so mindlessly, that he slipped time. Cataleptic afternoons became hung-over mornings: the coffee quest to warm shivering hands or to steady himself after an aborted sexual trauma. He sniffed his fingers for the residue of roasted Colombian beans, dried quim, cigarettes he didn't smoke. Fine ash, flakes of pastry, pubic hairs on a white saucer.

Thinking about it later, or before, planning it as a passage of prose, he couldn't be sure if it was the same night, probably not, after the Axel Turner retrospective in the National Portrait Gallery; walking rapidly away from, escaping, the fool who wanted him to record one of his dreams. As if. As if they could be separated, unplaited, one drearily bizarre episode detached from all the rest. The story from the story-teller. As if he were about to announce himself as a public liar. A pander. A pimp on the psyche. A hack. A grubber so deluded with self-importance that he would work for nothing, gratis, publish without payment. A thief, a leech. A man of letters. A whore who would scrape any sheet for the pleasure of seeing his name in print.

He fucked up. Beetled into a cul-de-sac and there was no way out. Norton's eyes, on these forced marches, roved endlessly. They were barely attached to his brain. They travelled the cracks in the paving stones, they flicked over walls. They caressed the outlines of buildings, absorbing them into his peculiarly selective address book. They snatched at faces, details of faces, hands, coats, rings, gloves, bags, the cut of a jacket, the way dark hair fell across the neck, or blonde hair lodged on a dirty suede collar. Gestures, frozen and replayed. They grazed headlines, the come-on poetry of newspaper sellers' posters. *World's Oldest Comedian Is Dead*. And not before time, Norton thought, suffering a rush of neon. An accountant of detail: he drank the city, in order to let it go.

Two men were standing in a puddle of inadequate light, waiting or posing, in front of a transgressive off-licence. Monochrome mates in a nightworld of unreliable colour temperatures. Black pores against a spill of expressionist halogen. Sick yellows, sorry reds. Windows to hawk products that required no selling. A booze shop, a rubber kiosk, an asthmatic who peddled cancer sticks. A 24-hour chemist. Ointments for incurable wounds. Jellies to ease penetration. Scarlet time capsules in beef-skin overcoats. Norton advanced, soliciting a hit. The shop, hidden as it was, unexpectedly encountered, promoted his unquenchable romanticism. He snaked tentative feelers towards a vial (the word was enough) of pale and smoky De Quincey liquor.

His tongue furred, erectile tissue anticipating the lick of heavy milk. Bug syrup. Blood that tasted of pear drops. Hallucinatory conceits stubbed out, extinguished by his censor motors. Norton would push past the pair of them, between them, enter the shop. There had to be a Chinaman inside, a hairless gook with dangerously arcane charts. The world understood as a system of symbols, symbolic values, valences. Impossible, at this distance, to tell if the night shop was open. Too late or too early. Days that were hopelessly out of synch. The walls of the court were tight against the shoulders of the two men. He had to look at them, at their faces, to consider how he would force a passage.

They weren't there. As he got closer, lifted his head, steeled himself to meet their eyes, or the eyes of the one on the right, the one who was staring at him – quizzical, sated, fraudulent – he saw that what he was confronting was no more than a sheet of paper. A poster. An inadequate copy, a tracing from one of the portraits in the exhibition. It was an advertisement, an off-cut. But it had decayed. Studying it, Norton stood his ground.

The sex shop behind him, it could never be altered now, reflected the poster. Two gentlemen of Soho: their weird intimacy, the one in a criminal raincoat, and the other, lounging against mirror glass, as if at a race meeting, invisible binoculars hanging from a white-cuffed wrist. Right hand in pocket. Left hand exposed, balled into a fist, fat as a frozen chicken. A barely tolerated pause in the curvature of their day: post-prandial, pre-sexual. Prepared to gamble: the risk of winning, the delight at throwing it away. Chucking bank notes on green baize. Prostituting the swift Mediterraneans who scooped up the dirty paper. Dog shit insults on crisp Belfast linen. What did the syphilitic playboys have to smile about? The poster was fogged and flawed, scratched, torn on one side, invaded by white. Put the end of your cigar to it and the men would disappear for ever.

The court had narrowed to a kind of box. Norton, what there was of him, was the light source, the bead of consciousness. He could only guess at what these men did. Did to each other. (He could, if pushed, allow his report to decline into fiction.) How did they pay for such expensive clothes? What were they waiting for? Their presence, Norton decided, was a filter between his exploitation of the city, the present moment, and De Quincey's immortal apothecary. The window of bottles and foreign labels, thin necks, queer colours, was alien, contraband. Shelves were arranged, when broken down in the bad reproduction of this poster, as Egyptian script. They said something. A crisis of hieratic animals and man-gods. The black coats of the two men spoke of funerals, funerary goods. One hit from the chemist's flask and Norton could join them.

'Without me, without what I'm seeing, this wouldn't be happening,' Norton decided. He had no part in the lives of these men. He understood, it was clear to anyone who spent time with the print, how they used each other, the nature of those private acts. Interchangeable rituals of domination and submission. What did not change was that one man paid and the other received payment. Gifts, ties, books he would not read, paintings he did not know how to sell. Chamber performances in a curtained room. Domesticity with a feral bias. 'Ready for your thrashing, Francis?' That's what Norton heard, invented. Polite Cockney. Airs and graces on the back landing. Proper family, pub-keeper posh. Stratford East. Road out. Staging post to Essex and drug baronial. Potential dog breeder. The sound of a leather belt slashing the cellar air.

The men weren't there, had never set foot in this court. Horizontal wine bottles racked alongside the man in the metal raincoat's kneecaps. Exterior was interior, an oyster bar. God, what brightly polished shoes! What disciplined loafers. Soft/hard. Architectural hair. The raincoat would pose in his underpants, suck in his belly, but he wouldn't take off his wrist-watch, his gold slave-chain. His patron, the one with the fleshy, Baggot Street face, the horse fancier, he dressed the London boy. Who had outlived his term of office. Face-down in the bog, gagging on turd water in an *en suite* bathroom. Flesh stripped to the bone, spinal cord pulsing like barbecued lizard. He dressed him, the exercised body, in women's things, black slips. Undergarments, wisps; beneath severe tailoring, top of the range schmutter. Dressed him as he fancied. As he would dress himself. As he had dressed, in the beginning. The start of it. In Chelsea, designing furniture, fabricating German interiors.

Norton couldn't, didn't want to, absorb this. The rush of illegitimate photo-flashes, the ruff of snapshots. It was all there, in front of him. Two men. One standing stiff, upright, ex-squaddie. The other: invertebrate. A slack V, a thin strip of the apothecary's window between them.

This was how the light behaved. It came off the dark poster, as from a reported event, an overheard conversation. It travelled towards Norton, through him, to bounce back from its own reflection. Revised by the place where it found itself. A conspiracy of the present into which Norton had stumbled. Light that had been roughed up in its passage. The photographer was dead. That much was obvious. A devious, streetwise innocent, a fall guy. The Irishman had paid for his funeral, bought him a hotel room in which to cough up his lungs. Paid for the X-rays. Listened, bored, to the hospital anecdotes. The transit of shadows. The photographer claimed his temporary immortality by stepping down, hoping that the two men would take him for a brandy, before going on somewhere the camera couldn't follow.

Without his concentration, the background to the double portrait begins to slip. The light, out of time, is sluggish, untested. The floor of the court sticks to Norton's feet. Heavy black shoes sliding on blood or paint. Rain. As from a sprinkler system. He can't hold the image. Hong Kong, snake-oil. Somebody else wants it. Somebody else is in the gallery, talking, commenting, re-narrating, revising the original occasion. The photograph, like all photographs, is a rehearsal. It will be better next time. In a parallel world.

The court begins to resent the poster. Other things happened here. Killings, affrays, telephone blow-jobs, brickwork polished by heaving mock-suede, buttock abrasions. Swamp rage, packets of powder. Stuffed with feathery ash, the two men simper. Lacquered in denture fixative. Beehive stiff, old queens. As light leaks like overspill. As slow waves fold into Norton. The poster and the reflection of the poster. Further and further apart. Floor stretched. Heavy sky pressing. The men tired of their pose. Tired of afternoon haircuts, razors scraping the back of the neck. Starched white shirts, silk underwear. 'Which side does sir hang?' Succulent lips, maggoty mind-sets.

No way of stopping it. The poster would have to be comprehensively understood, every crease of it: wood grain running into thumb-print. Pores that leak death. Smears and scrapes. Left too long in the bath. Worked over by technicians. Peg marks where the print was hung to dry.

Too late: the postcard in Norton's pocket is touched and fondled. It must divert a bullet aimed at his heart. The photographer photographed. Light sucked in, dragged towards the flaring match-head, the white lacuna of a cigarette. B-feature fag mag poses. The slash of a complimentary jacket across the groin. Eyes tired as glacial sand.

All dead, stopped. Suicided. Karma of wealth. Credit. Norton holds on to that bar of light, the phantom cigarette. The cylinder. Dismisses the rest. Slides between twin husks. Odours released on touch: garlic and tomato paste, fatty lamb, squid in its own ink. Chianti bottles nested in straw. Music and talk spoiling the street. He exhales, lets it go. Smoke borrowed from the dead photographer streams from his nostrils. A wisp of blue climbing into the darkness. A grain of tobacco lodged in his yellow teeth.

living with RA

19   65
IN A GARDEN
HOUSE ON THIS
SITE - DESTROYED
IN AN AIR RAID ON
18TH AUGUST 1940
HENRY JAMES
WROTE MANY OF
HIS NOVELS

p t o r s

(OR,

X

(OR, the missionary position)

The perfect recluse.
the missionary position)
The suicide who is still alive.

Peter Whitehead

living with RAptors
(OR, the missionARy position)

The perfect recluse. The suicide who is still alive

Peter Whitehead

*P*assion is always difficult. Writing about it. Discussing it in retrospect, when the damage has been done, and the immune system circumvented. Pytchley was dizzy, each step on the damp grass a test of memory. He lurched, stretched out his free hand, felt for a solid object to break his fall. The ground was untrustworthy. He was a revenant in his own park. That's what being away from London did. Travel disorientated him. The return home was the worst journey in the world. But, in his present condition, there was nowhere he would rather be, the bosom of his family, the chatter of his daughters. Webs of bird-spit glittered in the trees, delicate traceries provoking quietly erotic seizures. Country itches: the frottage of uncircumcised cockhead on muddy corduroy. The drench of horse-droppings on tarmac, steaming industrial slurry. Where better to initiate a slow convalescence?

It was confusing, those lost hours, not knowing who he was, what mask he should adopt. Coming back out of the black hole, the little death of anaesthesia. Like sex, he thought, you never return to the same body. He'd watched the dance of candlelight, backs broken, bent to one shape; watched himself, watched his partner; seen himself through her eyes; herself through his. He'd hovered and he'd swooped. Thrashed, branded. Licked the lush, suppurating wounds as if they were his own. Who *was* he now? This early morning walk would not settle it. Peter Pytchley: author, dramaturge, collector of curiosa, Egyptologist? Or Alan Wolfehead: Secret State spook, fixer, psychic hitman? 'Pete the Porn' or 'The Falconer'? Village shaman? Art gigolo? High Arctic adventurer? Dope smuggler? Shape-shifter? Elective gentleman? Pytchley, Wolfehead. Wolfehead, Pytchley. The names echoed and re-echoed to the spike and suck of his shooting stick, the drag of his dead heel. Guilty of everything. Nameless. Conscious of nothing beyond this circumference of pain.

The countryside was so loud: the whine of traffic, out on the arterial road, hurtling back to town. The carcinogenic singe of electricity swooping through the cradle of high voltage wires. Shotguns bringing down rooks. Man-traps. Chattering gossips. There were no buildings to buffer these inane interferences, to blanket his annoyance. The silence, out here, was rapacious. It fed on the hurt of his breath, the febrile hammering of his heart. No time left. Time marching through the repaired chambers like squadrons of Edgar Allan Poe gold bugs. 'I'm lost,' he muttered, 'my soul has drawn back to its virginity.' Unearthed on goat-cropped lawns, he sweated sharp crystals of fear. Disembodied in the sting of post-operative replays, he couldn't keep the night-thoughts in their cage. Sounds from the cutting room, chance remarks, a running tap. How they invoke the grind of the drill, the saw splintering dry bone. The cracking of ribs.

He walked, he limped. Where was he? There wasn't another property in sight. He could have been anywhere. That was his choice, his preferred life style. His wife, an artist, preoccupied with her own work. The current mistress straining at the barre. Or scoring a Voodoo jig. Nocturnals. Evening people. People who kept to their delegated quarters, meeting only for meals in the spacious, light-dappled kitchen. Meals that his wife would prepare. Francophile social arrangements on a pre-revolutionary Russian estate. *The Cherry Orchard* revamped by L.F. Céline. That's how he thought of it. As he hammered at the Bechstein grand. Sombre fugues of his own composition. God, he had magnificent hair. From blond to silver overnight. The traumas of genius. The agony of stalled composition. Eyes cold as stone. Skin like under-franked papyrus. Trembling hand. When no one watched him, his fires died. His shoulder dipped beneath a burden of remembered feathers. Bird-come running from the brim of his curious black hat. The curse of intelligence: seeing the multiverse as it really was. The energy fields, the rigorous elegance of scientific description. Systems of disbelief. His project? To stay alive and stay sane. *Stay* sane?

No more hallucinations, extended sick leave. No chemical forcing, no dubious mushrooms. The dream was as valid as any other part of the script. An equal, not an alternate, reality. This morning air, the sound of snail shells crunched by the beaks of thrushes, was his fantasy. English ground. Mellow brick, thatch, Virginia creeper. Cats stalking small vermin. A brain-damaged lurcher banging its snout against a dry stone wall. Boots that spilled desert sand. Pytchley had the soul of a Bedouin. And most of the *Oxford Book of English Verse* by heart. Yeats, Hopkins. Fellow birdmen. And Francis Thompson. The city would never leave him while he had the puff to recreate Thompson's morbid labyrinth.

His task? To balance the millennial elements, narcissism and melancholy. The troubled silence of drowned fields. Lamplight in his wife's workroom. The established English are so good at avoiding each other. He walked, letting the fugitive sentences take form. Like Henry James in Lamb House, with his oval circuit, one turn of the walled garden, lawn to amphitheatre to stable-block, a long-breath paragraph. Like James, the hesitation, the sleeve brushed across the eye, at the pets' graveyard. The empty falcon cages. The breeding pens. He staggered. His bowed legs spearing the wet grass like a pair of bent compasses.

The strength went out of him. He rested on a broken pillar. And saw – the old eidetic faculty was still active – the startling carmine lips of a Vargas pin-up floating in the green depths of a box hedge. Lips to inspire a Dali sofa. Lips that could shovel snow. A resting sex muscle, a labial erection. Wet, pouting, unsatisfied. Cartoon rinds so pumped with collagen invitation it was an offence not to dive straight into them, head first. And the teeth? White as shock, the afterburn of skull-bursting migraines. White as absence, nothingness. The impossible pearl dazzle of hyper-real adverts, where time implodes. And eternities are exhausted in a scatter of over-active microseconds. Computer generated claps of the eye.

Pytchley, a trained physicist, was impressed by the demonstration. Or, more properly, expressed by it. Self-demonstrated to an extent that made it impossible for him to move. He had two shooting-sticks to cope with. His eyes had fused into a single stalk – which threatened to split its socket. He had not thought himself capable of this. Not in his present state, the touch of embalming fluid still potent in his veins. It's strange when your thighs have been rerouted to your heart. You don't know if you're hiking or peddling frantically to circulate lethargic blood. Each step is a lung-bursting orgasm. Each orgasm an explosion of black feathers. For years Pytchley had rehearsed, revised, his suicide scene. In the desert, in a mud hut in Pakistan, the Outer Isles – fending off demons with a falcon lure. The whistle of a decapitated pigeon whirled on a thong. He had written himself into pyramid chambers and unexplored spaces within crystals. He had died and died again. The dry retch of mescaline. Now this. This scarlet surge. The Dionysiac purification of sight. 'Hi, I'm Tronna. You don't know me. Not yet. But, mister, I sure know you.'

A voice from the bush. The grating shriek of the Mid-West. Corn-fed innocence. Poisonous milk shakes. Pure James: American virtue offering itself to the dust tongue of Europe. A necrophile embrace underwritten by pillows of sweet-smelling, hay-breathed cash. Pytchley was all too familiar with *that* scenario. But what was the bint doing in his garden? (Tronna had her own reservations. Fucking the spook would be like falling into a vat of discarded bandages. Spooning locusts. Being blindfolded while a warty toad was placed on the tongue.)

From the voice, Pytchley, an old pro, read the rest: the compulsory, shoulder-length peroxide swarm, the doughy bosom and the short legs. He could taste pink toxins of bubble-gum. Such creatures, in truth, were outside his experience. He modelled this materialised wet dream on playbacks of Hank Janson (who he had never read).

Trouble was, the woman was doing an equal job on him. The silver-tongued, hawk-profiled English gent. An Englishness that could only be achieved by Low Scots, potato-bashers and too cultivated Hungarian Jews. Pytchley came from the era before all Hollywood Englishmen were sadists, culture Nazis. Tronna had the bite, the steam, that the neurasthenic dilettante lacked. The vampire in him sniffed her shoes.

He was unsurprised, incapable of it. He rewrote the world, on the spur, to accommodate uncanny, ill-disciplined showers of blood, fireballs over ancient stone circles, brown bathwater. 'Ah yes, I did that.' A terrible burden for anyone to bear. Holographic consciousness. Self and double. So she, this creature stepping forward, tottering on absurd heels, was an avatar of all the others. The glamour girls, strippers, dancers. He had summoned her, this lacquered initiator of onanism. A dragged-up masquerade of his anima, his female part.

You have to be properly incarnated before you can be reincarnated. He prepared himself for absorption by this advancing mass, the harlot-madonna in the lurid raincoat. So extreme was the punning self-parody of the Scarlet Woman that the beast in him suspected a Divine Director with a sense of humour. Colour so eager and shiny that it poked a finger in his eye. The red wrap arrived, creaking at every wiggle, seconds ahead of the creature who modelled it. Inky eyelashes curled into questions, sixes, Crowleyesque signatures.

'You the guy screws crows?'

That voice again. Rats in a blender. Car alarms parroting mandarin. He twitched as she thrust a gilded magazine into his face. A puff, a gloriously overwritten profile. Pytchley and his women, his falcons. His obituary.

'Says here you co-pu-late with guy falcons and finger fuck the chicks.'

'That's gyr, pronounced "jur". Gyr falcons. The most precious and sacred birds in the natural world. And, yes, the males express over my hat and my boots. And I introduce their semen, on my fingers, into the vulvas of receptive females.'

'Gross. That is truly gross. Can you show me?' Tronna hoisted a scarlet camera. A scream of plastic that matched her raincoat and her painted talons.

'Please.' But it was too late. The flash blinded him.

'Sorry, Pete. That's for definition. Get some life into your face. This country is just so godawful, pardon me, grim. Like the lights are out, period.'

What Tronna was after was the godlike beauty of Alan Wolfehead, Pytchley's earlier self – as revealed in this magazine plant. A full-page spread, hawk on wrist, mistress at shoulder.

'I had to come, Pete. As soon as I touched those pages. You were the living seed of Jesus.' Tronna, clutching his arm and dragging him back towards the sanctuary of the house, the open doors of the kitchen, gifted him with the story of her life. Unexpurgated, uncut. Triumphs and tears. He was her trophy, all that silver-mint hair. She wanted to carry him back to Mom in a picnic basket. The bleeding head of John the Baptist. And in exchange? She whispered in his ear. There was no between. She shouted like a cattle boss or she tried for girly and coy, breathless with naughtiness. When he filmed her, he'd have to find a way to make sure she kept her mouth shut. The banality had him blushing for shame, that he was capable of such an ugly fantasy. Because there was no way he would accept that this could be happening. Not to Peter Pytchley. Not in the English countryside as he knew it.

She'd crossed the pond as a tambourine smacker. From Salt Lake City or wherever. A god whore to one of those Orals. A come-on girl backing a margarine-haired messiah. A door-stepper. A light-in-the-eyes, tingle-in-your-lap babe. A 'yea' sayer. Tough as teak. If you didn't convert, sign over your tithe, she'd beat your brains out with her bible. A many times, born-again virgin.

Wolfehead, as she read about him, cried out for saving. Dragging down to the river. That boy had the emaciated body, the holy mane of the crucified Christ. And, in the Lord's name, she was going to nail him. She wasn't so sure about the transmogrified form, this Pytchley. More like punctured salvage from the tree. Holes in the palms of his hands. The whiff of the cave still seeping from his oxters. But his voice – oh, oh, that voice! – it had her purring like a coyote on heat in a truckstop corral.

Pytchley, liking the sounds her coat made, the protective shell of the woman, had no such problems. Daughter. One of his daughters. From the West Coast trip, surely? After that little misunderstanding with Orson Welles. The restaurant tab that was still in dispute. He might forget what the mothers looked like, but all his women fell into two types: artists and dancers. Sculptors who took themselves off out of it, to their capacious studios. Slim stunners who photographed limestone heads in museum basements. Object makers with a private income. And then there were the ballet girls, the Isadora Duncan types who could work up a death dance from a tape of his jazz-funk music. Exhibitionists who anticipated his every whim. Chicks who spread their own cheeks. Soho casuals whacked out in drug-dependency clinics and unreconstructed Northampton madhouses.

Tronna, as she admitted with a simper, *had* been a kind of dancer once, before she was saved. Exotic. Laptop. The kind of gal politicians and movers went for. That Clinton, why, he'd had so many complimentary blow jobs he looked like an inflatable. Like Ronald McDonald.

Excellent. Pytchley, testing her with his full weight, had found his latest blonde. There had been so many. And all the same. He had spoke of the double helix, the caduceus, spiral galaxies. How he had assisted Crick, tutored Sheldrake, penetrated the mysteries of X-ray crystallography. He helped her hand towards the lump in his pocket, the blood-red stone he was never without. 'But we'll speak of these matters another time, my dear. We have used enough of my vigour for today.'

Passion's difficult, I guess. But this Englishman is one strange *hombre*, know what I'm saying? That voice. It comes right at you – like Sir Anthony Hopkins. Remember? Hannibal Lecter, down there in the slammer, when he just *knows* what scent Jodie's dabbed on, how she's dripping with fear and whatever. He can snort yesterday's panties. Well, this Pytchley guy's like that. He understands, umm, right where you live. Spooky, but kind of sexy too.

And his hair! I want it. I want to take a bath in that stuff. It's long like a faggot rock star and it shines, and you can, umm, tell he's never had to work the streets in his entire life. His hands are smooth as a baby, a sex killer. Taking a cab out of town was the best move I ever made. It *is* passion, kind of. Obsession, anyhow. I gotta have him. Get him on film. I believe that. I do. I have witnessed the light. And he's made of it.

I wouldn't let him know it, but I could just eat him alive. Gobble him up. I swear I could. But I have to take it slow, real easy. Can't scare him. Let him talk and talk and talk. Talk himself right out. Talk out the devil and come on back to the arms of Jesus. The joy of the sinner that repenteth. And he's going to repent, baby, repent until he dies of it.

I'm wet. He's got me so wet I'm splashing the bathroom floor. I can hear him, right from the little girl's room. He won't stop talking. I want to sit on his face. That evil, holy voice. A shower of silver coins falling into the deacon's dish.

His aura was remarkable, a purple nimbus flickering to blue. Cold. The man was ice. She watched him openly, without disguise. He had stayed in control, he was driving. But so slowly. Taking such care. As if any movement of the wheel threatened to tear out the platinum stitches of his heart. And light flooded over them both. Now he saw her, now she was gone. Reds and golds and silvers. The nightworld of the road. She had persuaded him back to London.

This was a mistake, a kind of death. A reincarnation as Wolfehead, as state approved hack, double agent. Instrument of fate. The capsule of the car was not moving, the world moved gently against it. Now Tronna talked, rested her hand, for emphasis, on his knee. She became, in that warm darkness, the dancer. He listened, sympathised, entered her narrative. Shared it. Provoked it. He *was* Tronna. Himself, herself. The old man, Tiresias, in exile as a temple prostitute.

She was stroking him through the tweed. Yes, Wolfehead rising. American women smelt different. Soaped, showered, shaved. And the meat under it. The sweetness of the meat. She was hot in her plastic. He was collaborating in a ritual suicide. Whatever he thought, in the hallucination of the on-coming headlights, became the script. He tightened his grip. Kept his speed to a rigid forty miles per house. Did his breathing. The landscape was hunched and submissive, sliding him back to his earlier self, the pre-heart attack metropolitan. The man who squired Arabs around gambling clubs. The chronicler of the counter-culture. The spy, the manipulator. The energy thief. The dude who *really* made those stag movies. The Donald Cammell to Chris Petit's Nicolas Roeg.

He wasn't familiar with the east side. He'd always said that he was. Connected. Running with the gangs. On terms. But that was part of the front. He was lost. He could have been in Moscow. She worked him. Guided him through this wilderness of scrub-woods, snuff ponds, ethnics, grease caffs. He had died again. On the slab. Lea Bridge Road, that channel between the living and the immortal dead. The straightened labyrinth with its waxwork guardians.

Conjugations of stars – the night was crisp and sharp – shifted from pub sign to windscreen. And back again. The Pleiades. He remembered, invented, an earlier death plan: in a secret pyramid chamber. Essence into starlight. As she made him drive the dusty vehicle into a car wash. Black men who didn't have the language. White teeth. Scrubbing and hoovering. Tubes and soft yellow cloths. Big brushes blocking it all out. A rush and swoosh of water jets. Tropical rain. Not driving now. The car sliding forward of its own volition.

She takes him in her mouth. Everything scoured, made clean. Polished. He gushes milk into her open hand.

Everyone says Hoxton is one of the sharpest districts in which to live. Well, anyhow, I do. I say it. And I ought to know, I've been here for almost three weeks now. The London *Evening Standard* says so too, because I've got this article cut out and framed on my wall. Hoxton is like, umm, SoHo used to be. Artists and lofts and all kinds of native crafts and industries. They got delis and bars that open for breakfast, and clubs, and it's real close to the St Paul's church and the river and all that stuff . . . I've never actually lived in New York City, but this is as close as you can come. The smart designers and fashion models on bicycles and pavement cafés with poets. Pete's never been down in these slums, so I got the whip hand. It's my turf.

Now, I've got a teensy confession to make. I'm working on a screenplay. And, yeah, it's kinda based on my own experiences. And, boy, have I had some. Pete, he fits into this, real neat. I'm not expecting to hook some big movie deal, not out of the blue. Not first time. I'm writing it, if you want to know, to see how the story turns out. To see what happens to me, what the future is going to bring. 'Cos Pete explained that all writing is prophecy. You get it straight and it's bound to happen. Words have a kind of magic.

So, I shape what went down, make it over, recall it the best way I can, and this voice takes charge. Not me. The voice of the story. I can just barely keep up when it hits its stride. I'm in it. Pete's in it. Sometimes, umm, his wife, I guess. Real elegant. Beautiful long, high-class legs. French or European, right? Waxed not shaved. She digs me. She's a pure delight to know.

Hold on. I'll tell the story. Then it will happen. It has happened. It's happening now. I'm helping Pete up the stairs. I've caught him. He doesn't know where he is or what he's doing. He's lost the script.

How would I cast the picture? Gabriel Byrne, he could play Pete – but not as well, you bet, as Pete would do himself. I mean, Pete's such a natural aristocrat. So gracious and intelligent and fine spoken. Gabriel's good, but he's Irish. And too much of a hunk. Pete's appeal is more subtle. Like you can tell he always knows just what you're going to say, what you're thinking. All the real blushful stuff.

A younger Madonna would be good for my role, but it's too late now, with the baby and all, for that. I'll have to play it myself. See where it goes.

The loft she had was perfect. Quite surprising. It would have surprised a less informed intelligence. Not Pytchley. The black walls. The framed photographs. Polished glass to reflect the viewer. To marry voyeur and object of desire. The spook had been here before, many, many times. It was his set, the interior of the dark crystal, the Egyptian tomb. It was where he played out his psycho dramas, where he released his demons from the aether. Where he contacted the spirit of the bird, of Horus. Where he returned to himself after a liberating voyage through time and space. Where he made sacrifice.

He was tired. The drive had drained him. He allowed himself to be led across the shining floor to the great brass bed. He subsided, saw himself doubled, reversed. A floating other trapped in the bordello mirror. Wolfe-head floated over Pytchley. It was too much. Heart pounding. The operation had been botched, something alien left in the wound. He was dying again. Tipping backwards into darkness, spilling his lifeforce. Into the feathers. Into sleep.

Whap! The flashbulb was so close it scorched his eyebrows. She was at it again, logging him. He thrust out his jaw, ironed the folds in his neck. Tossed his hair. She bent forward, a puff of talcum powder, the soothing touch of her hand. So warm. As she slipped the blindfold over his weary eyes. Angel of Death. Healer, killer. Agent of release. 'I'm being raped by images,' Pytchley thought. TV replays, barbecued monks. Napalm. Assassination. He went for the big stuff. As he heard the bulbs pop, he conjured up waterfalls that blew back over sheer cliffs. The oldest rocks in the world. Deserts that stretched for ever in the mind. Volcanoes. Drifts of bombs. Torched ghettoes. 'Images must become instantly forgettable, or we will all go mad! We are conditioned to be blind.' In his nightmare, he was unpicked. Layer by layer, print by print. The more she discovered, the less he knew. She cuffed his wrists to the bedhead. 'Who am I?' he screamed.

He had the cutest scar you've ever seen. A Nile, a relief river, running straight down his chest and most of the way across his firm belly. Not a hair to be found. Still shaved from the operation and not grown back. But he had, as she discovered, uncoupling his suspenders, shaking him out of his trousers, something else – a curious chastity belt, a corset. Around his waist was this off-white, sweat-stained, shamanistic, Joseph Beuys garment.

What was its purpose? She ran her hands over the porous material. Was it something to do with his operation? Did it hold him together? There were pouches sewn into the belt, big enough to carry limestone pebbles, or bullion bars. Phials of drugs. Microfilms. 'My eggs. Don't touch my eggs.' He surfaced from his reverie, heard himself speak. The woman was fiddling with his egg belt, trying to find the catch. Pytchley as an incubator of falcons. Pytchley travelling back from Iceland to Morocco. His associates always spoke of his 'cool'. Nothing phased him. He breezed through border posts. The belt was his pregnancy wrap, he mothered birds that he had also sired. Father and mother, both. Eggs, in a cheesy belt, held against the warmth of his belly. Like the skin, a sculptor once told him, of a man who has been turned inside out. Globules of fat decorating the peeled cast. Eggs of body sweat. Glistening lard trophies.

Blindfolded, Pytchley saw – imagined – too much. Tronna became his Antigone. The old myths are the best myths. Leading him to his doom, favourite daughter. 'I am your eyes, Daddy. I have come to guide you through the abandonment of the city.' Blindness excusing the incest prohibition. Blindness letting him see. The thongs she had on his wrists and ankles became, perversely, the instruments of his freedom. Not responsible, he could respond. Control, direct. Unable to move, he would inspire movement in others.

He'd expected the cuffs of a nurse's uniform, not the black of a nun. He was back in the hospital, Arabs setting their fires in the corridors. Tethered goats. Not incense and angel music. Wrong tape. The adhesive she was fixing over his mouth. He's trussed like a chicken.

Photographs. It had to be done in photographs. I saw Pete as a book first, then, who knows, if I got lucky, a major exhibition. Somewhere like, oh, that Slaughterhouse Gallery place, down in Smithfield, the old meat market. Berkoff had shown there and plenty of other celebrities. You could, maybe, have the prints upstairs, all along the wall, in sequence – and then you'd be led to the brink, to where you look over the abyss, down into the cellars. And a spotlight would pick, out of the darkness, Pete's skin hanging on a hook. Early days, but something like that, you know, could be pretty dramatic.

He likes showing himself, you can tell. He's got plenty to show, he's in shape for an old guy. Flash! I do an establishing shot. The torso. All of it. I'll leave him for now with those white stockings. Surgical supports, I guess, where they took the veins to use in his heart. But the legs are good and if I can arrange them properly, he'll come over kind of kinky, trans-sexual. Flash! One more from the other side.

I taste the skin of his shoulder. Cold as death. I want to trace all those wounds with my lips. Map him. Flash! An icon. One of the martyred saints. The ridges of his scars are physical features in an undiscovered city. A mysterious continent seen from space. Get right in on those puncture holes. Flash! Whatever I frame changes the fate of the city. He has to live up to these beautiful prints. And by dying again, if that's what it takes.

From the street you could see the pulsing window. The instants of illumination. The woman moving backwards and forwards against the uncurtained rectangle. A frame of cinema. And with each starburst, Pytchley sank deeper into his trance, willed her on, solicited the prick of the blade. The slashes that would heal his wounds by re-opening them. He was back at the point of the first attack, crawling towards a glass telephone. His hand reaching out for it. He was there as the first beams of sunlight crept over the lip of the balcony, the trees in the park. The returned suicide. The dead man who has crawled out of the river.

Tronna stood over him, stood back, walked around the bed. It was uncanny how the body absorbed light. Pytchley shone like an extra-terrestrial, a starman. It was as if each photograph punctured his carapace, let his spirit flood out. Every image had undone one block of the narrative. He was forgetting his story, escaping the tyranny of remembrance. Bound tight, wrapped like a parcel, he was a pupa. Between larva and imago. A shell secreted out of his own essence. An egg.

Pytchley couldn't have written it better. The brilliance of the lamps. He could see through the black cloth. How Tronna climbed up on to the bed, straddled him. The dead Osiris brought back to life by the hawk. Glamorous, necrophile. A sarcophagus Polaroid. What he'd always wanted, didn't they all? All men. To be mastered, forgiven.

What an unusual name, Tronna. He tried to speak it aloud, test its meaning. She pressed her lips against the vibrating tape. 'Not Tronna, honey. Tronno. T-r-o-n-n-o.' The letters burnt into his lids. They twitched and danced. Tronno. An androgynous being from a distant galaxy. From some downriver midden. The letters rearranged themselves into a more conventional form. A sound like London. *Norton*. His oldest enemy in her newest form.

Her hands tore at the cicatrix, the zipper of flesh. Reaching for the wet heart, the falcon. The light from the dark star. Empty pages. Human vellum. The last sentence swallowed in a gush of salt.

scrip.
scribe.

the imagery into which he taps.

This third graphic story takes a slightly different form

rly relate to the conventions of cinema. This time, I

hrenic relation to between text & image: as if they

ite integrate here will be blocks text

se continuity boxes

script. xi

He has already become proficient in the

habit of simulating that he was someone,

so that others would not discover his

condition as no-one.
JL Borges

Chapter 1
Scrip. Scribe. Script.

Green banknotes are the moss of the City. They convert our pockets to soft pouches. They cut our fingers. Lick them and we bleed. Banknotes are the thinnest passports, Norton claims, the membership cards that will let him on to the river.

I AM A CITIZEN.

A CITY ZEN.

Norton is cracking. The moon is his bent coin.
He is almost ready to reveal his face.

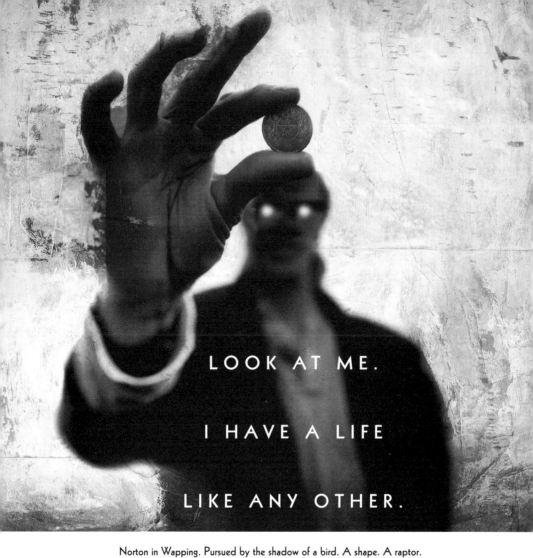

LOOK AT ME.

I HAVE A LIFE

LIKE ANY OTHER.

Norton in Wapping. Pursued by the shadow of a bird. A shape. A raptor. A thing squatting at the kerbside. Madness sits and sings. Madness hides behind lighted windows. Madness is his pet. He tastes its sooty fur.

Inside the lining of his funeral coat Norton has money. Skeleton man fat as Orson Welles. Lips closed on a tube of banknotes, a phantom cigar. He nourishes a cash pillow. Filched from the City. Dirt transactions: old books, new drugs. Killings, kitings, paper fraud. Norton. Sleeping rough in a wealth of unrealised royal promises. The Masonry of the dispossessed. Cash without credit won't light the fire.

Trace the watermark, the blue tributary. There's an old boy down here in the stews. He holds the key. An ex-mariner, India hand. A walnut-complexioned hunchback, face full of bad weather. Skin macerated in linseed solution. No oil painting, thought Norton. Pity he's too previous for Francis Bacon. Because they are all dead in the Ship & Bladebone, over-active corpses. Returned suicides.

The forger is Norton's last hope. Address supplied by the late Axel Turner, who shared the surname. The old soak could be the skinhead photographer's father. Also known as "The Admiral", "Puggy Booth", "Short-Arse". A boozer, specialist in lost weekends. Put a pewter tankard of sherry on the table, and he'll talk to you. Run off banknotes. (Sideline in exuberant sunsets, ape porn, bearded clams.)

Don't worry, son, we keep them sheeted upstairs.

There are only two things worth painting. Sunsets and cunts. When I bring them together, I'll die happy.

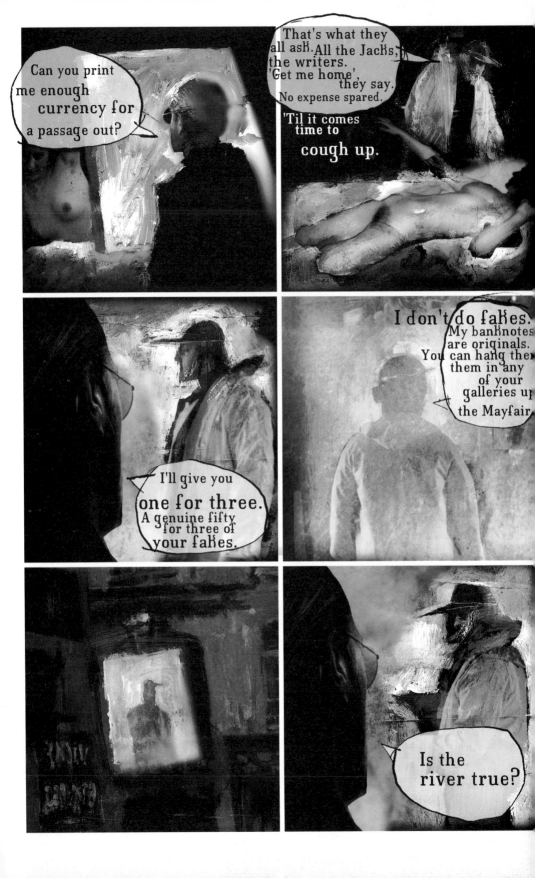

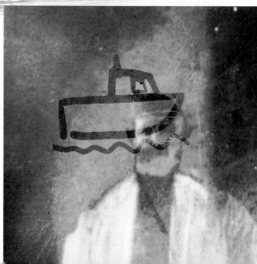

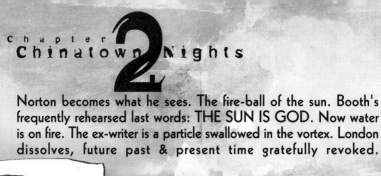

Chapter 2
Chinatown Nights

Norton becomes what he sees. The fire-ball of the sun. Booth's frequently rehearsed last words: THE SUN IS GOD. Now water is on fire. The ex-writer is a particle swallowed in the vortex. London dissolves, future past & present time gratefully revoked.

Dr Fu-Manchu figure, high up in one of the glass towers, watching the river.

All clues lead to the river.

(Alan Wolfehead again.)

e doctor, as in all the movies, is obviously a European, an Englishman in ncy dress, with a long string moustache & painted eyes. (Alan Wolfehead ain.)

The crew of the Reliance demand wine, rum, cigars, shell-fish. Tottie. Provisions for the trip. Fuel. Charts. Burwell rhapsodises Macao, Casablanca, the Congo. But has, in reality, never achieved Leigh-on-Sea. Burwell wants cash.

Half now and half on landfall.

Norton ashore. Already tainted by the river, he staggers. His sea-legs are like tins of Special Brew stuffed into surgical stockings. Many of the glass towers are burnt out, with plasterboard windows. Shrouded in flapping canvas.

NOVA KONG. Norton in quest of the Chinaman. They're all here now, the fiscal runaways. Money laundering in place of the traditional steam-presses. Credit where no credit is due. The Island. Everything you want except the shop.

Schizo consciousness. City split. City within a city. Norton divided between a Wong Kar-Wai travelling shot, down into the bowels of the earth, all sweat-vest gamblers, smokers, food stalls, neon spill - and the antiquarian picaresque of Thomas Burke and Sax Rohmer. Chinatown Nights. Fabulous opium dens. White women gone to the bad. The savage perversions of the Orient. Dogs' heads simmering in woks. Triad assassins with gold teeth. Dragon tattoos. Books of wisdom printed on skin.

It never changes. The same old equation: cash, dope, credit.
Every doctor selling cures for diseases that do not yet exist.
Viral colonisation. Who controls currency controls life.
The green tide. The alchemy of sunset.

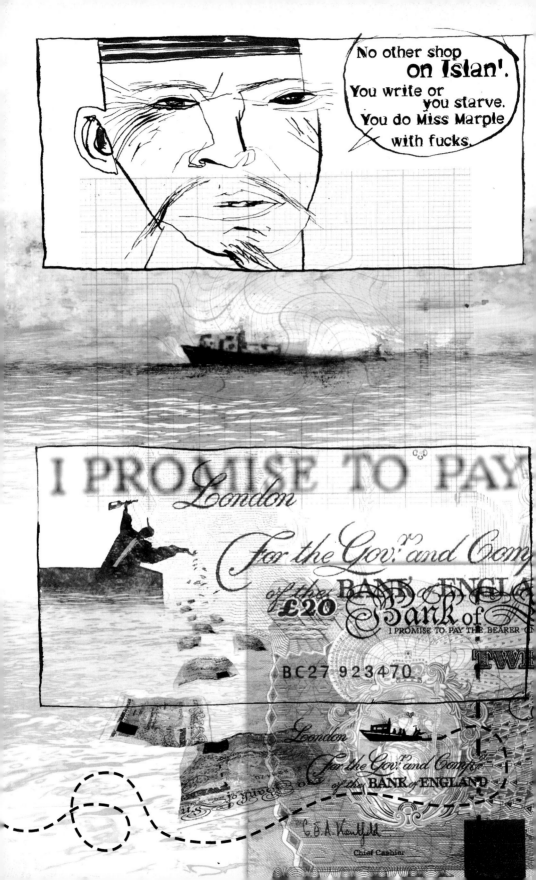

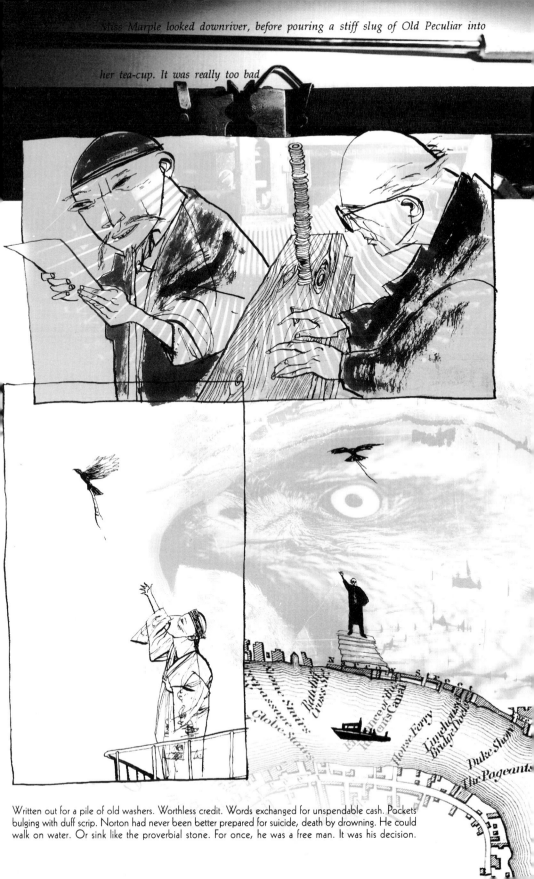

Miss Marple looked downriver, before pouring a stiff slug of Old Peculiar into

her tea-cup. It was really too bad

Written out for a pile of old washers. Worthless credit. Words exchanged for unspendable cash. Pockets bulging with duff scrip. Norton had never been better prepared for suicide, death by drowning. He could walk on water. Or sink like the proverbial stone. For once, he was a free man. It was his decision.

He is on the return path from his walk towards the fire.
M. Heidegger

The Contents **XII** of the Kettles

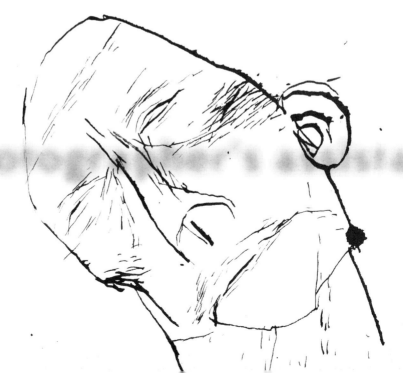

the contents oꜰ the kettles

He is on the return path from his walk towards the fire

M. Heidegger

*T*here are days, downstream of the barrier, when consciousness is contained within an opaque envelope, a membrane of
river mist. When the marshes move out of time and the bones of
the Dartford bridge – why do they call it a tunnel? – loom like the skeleton
of a dinosaur. Beams from dead eyes sweep in an aerial procession.
Electricity is generated in swamplands. You can hear the fat cables hiss
and spark.

Norton floated. Knees to chin. Giving the rain a smaller target on which
to work. Deptford to Dartford. He was inside an egg or a bubble. He drifted
over the choppy river. He had made it, fulfilled his contract. He was on his
way out. He remembered this place, summer, a field of poppies. The open

door of the car. A woman in a tight yellow sweater. The yellow and the red. Lifting her arms. His mouth on hers. The aftertaste of whisky. A thin silver necklace disappearing between her breasts. He remembered hot dust stinging his eyes as he spread his jacket on the ground. He remembered what had never happened.

The Photographer

It goes without saying – if he's alive, I'm dead. Crow meat. But I swear that it's me inside that egg. And it's not opaque. I can see: the river, the bridge, all those demented locations I shot for him. I'll tell it. Tell it as it was. No embellishments. No language.

He portrays me as a dummy, but that's bollocks. Lazy writing. He's got nothing to go on except my height, the stubbled skull, the earrings, the tattoos. Any idiot can do better than that. Any comic strip hack. And now? When all the trappings have gone? He's jacked it in. He drops me from the script.

I read as much as he does, more. Tougher prose. I read what I find. What I'm given. Petit leant me a copy of Gaston Bachelard's The Poetics of Reverie. Norton couldn't go near it. Poetry and pulp, that's his limit. He should dip into this stuff. He might learn something. 'For those of us who can only work on written documents, on documents which are produced by a will to "edit", a certain indecision cannot be obliterated in the conclusions which terminate our inquiries. In point of fact, who writes? The animus or the anima? Is it possible for a writer to carry his animus sincerity and his anima sincerity through to the very end?'

Snap! Let the bugger chew on that one. Who writes? Who's got the copyright on Norton's fiction? I've seen him provoke conversations in grease caffs, just so he can find out where the story leads. He's a stenographer, not an artist. A tape machine. And he's been using me all along, because he's too fucking incompetent to describe landscapes or buildings without a prompt. His memory's crap, to tell the truth. Check out any of his yarns and you'll see what I mean. He's a phony. Bullshit from arse to tip.

OK, I've got the bastard sussed. But where does that leave me? I'm something he invented and then chucked away. A couple of frames in a paranoid fable. But it doesn't stop there. The story moves on, even when he's too preoccupied with his career to record it. The sites I've photographed survive their destruction. I have an entire city boxed beneath my bed. I dream on these leaking plates.

Listen to my version, if you want the truth. We came down early on the train and scored — by following a bunch of hardhats — a surprisingly good breakfast alongside Abbey Wood station. I rated it eight out of ten. He was scribbling in his notebook, while he spooned the mess of broken yolk with his free hand. He said he couldn't understand how they'd let us through. We'd never been so far from London. This was somewhere else entirely.

We had to check the river. My photographs are the only record. Thamesmead, one of the dim places of the earth. Unpeopled. Retro futurist. Stagnant ponds, walkways. Views into box houses. Bridges that overlook an abstraction of roads and road markings. Just Petit's kind of place, I told him. We'll have to come back one day. He laughed.

The silence had got to him. The dogs. He dragged us back inland, in search of some abbey ruins. That's when it started to get seriously weird. I'll tell you all about it. I'll give you the full . . .

McKean

I've run into a major difficulty. I've no idea what this character looks like. How am I supposed to draw him? 'Never see his face' the script says. 'Seen from behind. Long black coat. Balding.' That's about it. Which is fine for a couple of panels — but an entire book? Norton. He's a focusing device. There's no life in him. I never had these problems with Neil Gaiman. Neil's a pro. He could give me a couple of lines on the blower and I could run off the pages. We're on the same wavelength. But Norton's a disaster. All I get is packages of photographs. And not even that, photocopies of photographs. Photocopies and references to obscure movies, books that no normal person has the time to read.

What he doesn't seem to understand is that this is a job like any other. A deadline. Get it done. Move on. You're talking really about basic technical problems — how the page will break down into panels, the information in the continuity boxes, keeping the narrative alive. I can solve most things, fast, by applying the right technology. Book design, CDs, brochures, graphic novels, fine art. The right tools. A raid on the image bank.

I don't leave home if I can help it. Why should I? It's all here. This is the way the world's going: William Morris cottage industries serviced by top gun software. Studio life, that's the future. I can't sympathise with Norton. I suppose that's the crux of it. What's his problem? What makes him so restless? He moans about having to write. The guy's lucky to be offered the chance. Thousands would kill for it. The greatest city in the world. He should get married, settle down. Art's a career like any other.

180

Contacts are more important than inspiration. Forget ego. I always quote Lamartine:
'It is not I who thinks but my ideas which think for me.'

The other drag is that I work in golds and browns. I'm an autumn person: birds'
wings, dolls' heads, old maps, dry leaves. Norton is grey-blue, dead water. He's river.
I'm earth. He's foul air and I'm the afterglow of fire.

Lesnes Abbey is not worth a paragraph. Even though it oversees the splendour of Thamesmead. Norton embarrassed himself, stopping dog-women to enquire after 'Laines' Abbey. That was his Frenchified pronunciation, how he saw the letters of it. 'Lanes' Abbey was the sound he made. A choice of paths scuttling into scrub woods. (Petit's camera, if it had been present, would have spun in circles, like a demented heritage toy. A first-time director trying to pump life into a bosom and breeches drama. A mute *ingénue*, in focus, standing on the camera platform, as the background is whirled into a smear of colour.)

How the dog-women laughed. Cackled. Wet themselves. 'Les-nez' Abbey. 'Right behind you, mate.' That rim of sad grey bricks. Those municipal gardens. See the phantom towers of Thamesmead rise over the sward. See the early shadows. The drooping roses. Tell it, Norton. Tell it like it never was.

Is. Was. Whatever. Lesnes: inspirer of lost gospels. Lindisfarne of the boondocks. Fabulous beasts inked on vellum. Norton could go for that. Truly graphic fiction. Apocalyptic. Red-letter columns that stop the breath. Books that displace the weight of the world.

Norton squatted, taking in this scene: that he had, after so long, shaken free of London. The first day of the rest of his life. Light worshipper. It was almost enough, the clouds parting to spill a benediction of sunbeams. Norton Heliophyte. He blossomed. The panels of his bare skull split and parted. Nothing to be said, nothing to notice. The slaphead photographer searching ineffectually for a way to give significant form to this uninspired location. To make it reveal itself. 'Better to leave well alone,' Norton thought. 'Quit while we're ahead.'

The Photographer
I knew it. He wouldn't be able to resist the woods. One last fairy tale, end with a
flourish. It's the Dante in him. The way that all Yank horror films have to come up

with their compulsory epigrams from Il Purgatorio. *Midway through the schelpp of life. More than that, mate. On the downslope. Sniff the furnaces. The dark wood of the world. One more undiscovered country. Nothing like mixing your sources, cross-cutting, overloading the storyline. What story? It's a sequence of unconnected images: Thamesmead, its simmering mania, Lesnes Abbey, flowerbeds, hills blanketed with mixed woods. Ancient and modern. No text. Frame to frame. Walk through in any order you fancy.*

I keep these small flickbook albums and you'd be far better off relying on those. A railway bridge. The graffiti: HELEN IS A WHORE! *A Post Office with a queue of scroungers in anoraks and cheap leather jackets. That's how you can tell it's a Monday. Dole bandits and their wretched kids. Norton's too self-absorbed, too high culture, he'd never notice reality pissing on his boots.*

The path through the woods, described in the leaflet as a 'green chain', kept dividing. We went uphill in a vaguely westerly direction. I didn't know what he had in mind. The conclusion he was aiming for. We wasted an hour or so – light breaking through the canopy, nothing too dense, no claustrophobia – when we chanced on a black pond.

Do we go round it? Chuck stones? Or throw ourselves in? Your man wasn't in a talkative mood. We stood there. I guess he was expecting me to knock off a roll of film. But it wasn't that interesting, mud soup. Then a civilian – elderly, unbuttoned in a badly-fitting cardigan, and slippers – broke cover.

He started to jabber at Norton, quite excited, in a sort of French. Did Norton know Liège? I thought he said 'Lesnes'. But Norton boasted a few words from the phrase book. A Belgian, he said. A Belgian who had lost his motor. (His mama?) Another mislaid Alzheimer's case. A runaway that nobody wanted to chase. Too many cups of weak tea sapping his resistance. Too many sprouts in aluminium pans. Brussels sprouts.We let him go. Tears of agitation running down his cheeks.

'Even I couldn't fit him into the story,' Norton said.

The woods become, after the first couple of hours, a muffled interior. Great green cloisters. I will walk here a while, it's my breathing time of day. (Norton mused.) I let the boughs knot overhead. I put one foot in front of the other and leave it at that. Do I understand what the quest is? Has the narrative taken shape? All I know is that if we keep moving, chasing the declining sun, we'll arrive back at the outskirts of the city. Then a decision can be made. To pretend this never happened, revert to the familiar script, the same old paradoxes. Or to quit. Take a chance. Head off into the unknown – risking, no, insisting upon, annihilation. Dreamless sleep. Oceanic nothingness.

Lesnes Abbey Woods should, according to the chart, the laminated board (with its cancellations and red ink revisions), give way to Bostall Woods, various commons, unedited farmland, dense roadside verges. Falconwoods, I suppose. Most of our expeditions end there. A snapshot to send to Pytchley, as a provocation. Forensic evidence for his tin box. A nostalgic glimpse of the railway line. A turn around the graveyard. Cop cars on duty. Cop cars in the middle of unharvested cereals. Not us, not this time. Forewarned. Rehearsing the next child murder. Nailing down blue ribbon markers in the expectation of a road rage stabbing. Hunting redskins who have skipped the reservation.

So how about this? I'm weary, it's the best I can come up with. I'm out to locate the site of . . . Mount Whoredom. Somewhere in these woods – a tumulus, an earthwork, a mossy pyramid – there is a mound that disguises . . . that is made from a heap of skulls, bones. A clearing dedicated to the production of mummia, mummy flesh for ritual purposes. Mummified leather. Sacrificial victims buried in a heap. Eviscerated, wrapped in herbs, soaked in oils. Stuffed with sand. A cult of dangerous en-lightenment, loosely associated with Charlton House, Eltham Palace. Cannibalism. Deranged aboriginals wandering the paths, the circuits of this purgatory. As we are. Mud up to their ankles. In the dog woods. Under the whisper of oak and elm. Under beech and hawthorn. Under ash.

And this is why I poke my stick into likely tumps. Why I bribe Turner, with the promise of a fizzy drink and a bag of chips, to photograph arboreal anomalies. Growths on the bark. Mushroom flesh. Wool trapped in thorn bushes. Bloody rags. This is why I lick my fingers. Chew on sticks of spearmint. Wait for the hallucination to kick in. Why I finger the knife in my pocket.

The Photographer's Partner

Sod this for a kettle of fish. I'm taking a bath. And, believe me, living with Turner, that's a rare privilege. Even the shower has to be pre-booked. The shower room is never free of strips of film, trays of chemicals, prints pegged out to dry. Getting your kit off means meeting a mirror image of yourself on curled paper, means posing for another round of art snaps. We don't have a present. We have a rehearsal for tomorrow's duo tones. I have to live up to my documented double. Reinvent or risk redundancy. I'm in perpetual competition with my younger self.

With Petit out of town, motoring for a few days through the West Country, logging the frozen frames, laying down more sunsets, his flat is free. I have the key to his amazing en suite *bathroom. The tiles, the mirrors, the blissful depth of that tub. A sarcophagus with gold taps.*

Turner's skipped too. On the road. God knows where, dogging Norton. But here's the strange thing, I decided to give him a shock, do what he expected, change my look. Lay off the bottle, go black. Then stretch out with Petit's sun ray lamp in the black orthopaedic chair, get a bit of a tan. No more Nordic pallor. No choc bar zits.

Forty minutes might have been overdoing it. Goggles on. Saw myself in the glass and didn't believe it. Another woman altogether. Somebody I didn't recognise. The inky mop and the skin like blistered bacon. Which is why I decided on a long slow soak. And why it happened.

That's what I meant by strange. How, as soon as I shut my eyes, I saw Turner. With Norton. It wasn't a fantasy or a daydream. It was more like a film projected on the inside of the goggles. It was my story. I was the one telling it.

Warm soapy water. Lying back. A huge tooth glass of Petit's whisky. One of his Hamlets in my hand. Painted nails. Posing for a film that I was directing. Focusing on the details that took my fancy. Tasting the smoke, then letting it go. And the water was also the river. Was the trip out beyond Sheppey. Burwell giving his instructions, calling out the depths. My brilliant red nails on the chill wheel.

I tell you, it's my script. I'll get my sister to take the shot. Then see what I can do with laser copying, with process. Light alchemy. I'll call it Sol Niger, *out of Dante. Out of alchemy. Black sun of secret bathrooms.*

I can't be bothered. I let the story drift any way it wants. Reflections of branches in the water. It's getting cold. I play with the taps. I reach for them with my toes. The skin is tight on my face. If I touch myself, stroke the side of the tub, I feel hard granules of earth.

Success. They are completely lost. And: either it's getting dark or the overhead canopy is so thick they've found their way back into the pre-Roman forest. (Is 'back' the right word?) Nothing to go on. Norton thought of fire. He was up for it. Heat left in calx. Trees were conflagrations still to come. Flames scouring base desire. No traffic sounds. Howling dogs. More wolf, he fabled, than dog. Wolf and moon. Leaf mulch underfoot. The density of dying green and encroaching brown provoked an eloquent silence. What now? What trick? He was finished, out of ideas, tired of shorthanding himself. 'The soul as a stranger upon the earth.' Right!

Turner mute as an old shoe and about as fragrant. The forest was always there. How should it change? I'm no reincarnation of Marlowe, Norton thought, it's the other way around. Without me, there is no Marlowe. I sketch what he was. He relives the lines I feed him. His visions are what I misquote. I am his broken couplets. Norton sweated in the shadow of so many potential books. Oak libraries. Pine pulp. Brackish streams of vanity verse.

How soon then, if they continue to circle this mound, before they meet themselves? Before, labouring uphill, their path will be blocked by an identical pair. Other, better selves imagining them. And behind those? Regiments of dark-coated Nortons, battalions of Turners. Future and past. The word and the image, parasitical life forms. Pimping each other, talking each other down. The trees, in the gloom, would be men again. A forest of accusing voices.

'At least, looking on the bright side, we're out of the city.' Norton muttered. 'Away from the smoke.' No more London. Nothing to work on. No previous. Virgin territory. Which is why he was dumb. Why there was nothing for Turner to shoot. Between them, they couldn't name a single plant. Edible or inedible, they hadn't a clue. They didn't have the vocabulary for this set. Trees were trees and shit was shit. So could they, in truth, claim to be here at all?

Turn it over to McKean. That was Norton's first thought. 'Dear Dave – can you knock out a couple of pages of woodlands? Something of the atmosphere of Jack Trevor Story's *Trouble With Harry*, souped up with Anselm Kiefer. Boisterous gloom. Kentish hills, inland from Thamesmead. Do a bit of *Clockwork Orange* if you fancy it. Alienated adolescents in a dystopian moonscape. Norton and Turner as pilgrims. (Photos to follow.) Get the trees right. Magic mushrooms. (Try some yourself, if that helps.) Regular panels for once, script visible underneath. Then treat it to your usual shtick with lark skulls, crow beaks, maggoty wood shavings, steel wings, scarecrows. A couple of lines of moody text. Posy foreign quotes. You can do it blindfold. And Bob's your uncle. Cheque in the post.'

No use. McKean was tied up for months with real world projects. You'd never get him down here. He wouldn't leave the oast house for this featureless excursion. How could he pitch it to the Yanks? Try selling Norton to DC Comics. McKean couldn't even remember the title of the book from one day to the next. *The Breathing Time*. That was the first attempt – until the editors got hold of it. 'We like obscure, but we need obscure that the ordinary reader can understand. Capeesh? Hamlet? Shamlet. The reps won't buy it, so think again, buddy.'

Norton had to find another way to get them out of it. No use in passing the burden of narrative to Turner. He'd tried that one before. And Turner, without his spell-check, could land them deep in the wolds of Cunt. Harp-picking with larking cockknees. The photographer, let loose on a type-writer, would turn Dan T's *Infernal* into *Finnegan's Wok*.

They arrived, as is traditional, at a parting of the ways. The track bifurcated and offered an impossible choice. Another cruel V. Turner made the joke he always made: 'When you come to a fork in the road, take it.' Norton was also true to type. (What else? The geek was a cartoon.) He used his name as a method of divination.

Here's how it worked: at the first division, go north (N); next, straight on (O); next, turn back (T); then on again (O); and, finally, north (N). Fine, as long as that lasted. Two or three hours brought them to the rotting log from which they had set out. Norton who, in delusive confidence, had dumped his black satchel, now picked it up again. Nothing to eat or drink. Too dark to read. The track was still there.

Turner, pushing his luck, suggested that they try *his* name. A fraud, an invention, a threadbare counterfeit. Why not? Norton had run out of steam. T: turn – to the original compass bearing. Nothing original in that. U: the conservative strategy, spin on the heels, retrace your steps, but from a fresh perspective. (Norton swallowed his contempt.) R: off to the right, slithering up a muddy slope. This was more promising. Turner reckoned – septum shot to buggery – that he could smell wood smoke. They spotted a clearing ahead, a swampy declivity that might once have contained a small pond. Traces, Norton thought, of a broken camp. Hints of recent life, a couple of ancient kettles. Norton acid-flashed to the expedition sent out to track rumours of Sir John Franklin. High Arctic folly. Anglos, in the wrong landscape, driven to peck at their shipmates' scurvied flesh. Blinding visions brought on by forbidden meat. Crystalline patterns as sight shuts down. Another legend. Kettles are so domestic when you come across them outside a gallery environment. When their surrealism is innate, not exploited.

An alternative route was on offer. But they didn't have to involve themselves with these too literary prompts. They stood, shoulder to shoulder, debating the N. Turner took it – and it was, after all, his N they were talking about – for a firm negative. An oracular 'No'. Loud and to the point. But no, as Norton pointed out, to which question. Not on? Or not to step aside? And anyway, by the conventions they had already established, N stood for north.

'But which way is north?' Turner whined. ER was all that was left to them. Confusion, not a passport stamped by royalty. 'Er, um, right then.' Right? No. On. It's all the same. But it was time for action.

The first kettle, as predicted, had fatty deposits. Hardly convincing evidence of cannibalism, but worth a lick. A sniff. Rusty flesh. A taste that made Norton gag. This was where the skulls were boiled. Turner poked around the clearing for other signs. Light was creeping through the high boughs. It might have been a new day. Dawn changes everything.

They started to dig, scrape back the clammy topsoil, hoping for the worst. And that is what they found. Yellow mud, like a burst sewage pipe, webbed their fingers, poulticed their pores. Mud that smelled like spider pus. Lightless rooms that nobody had thought about for thirty years. Condom socks.

And, after the layer of superficial slime, pages that weren't paper and would never again be wood. White coal. Pages you couldn't read. Print that had been drained away. Leaves of unread books. A burst library tank that threatened to flood the gound with poisonous literature. The boundaries between fictions had been worn away. Narrative integrity was lost. Plagiarism outlasted its source. This was a dreadful place. This was where the archetypes got out.

Better to coat your hands with resin from the kettles. Make a cast. Remember memory. Remember to forget. Rub fat on flinching skin. Like the Eskimos who outlasted Franklin, that over-civilised man. Roll naked in the grease, until the curled leaves stick and make a coat.

Norton dipped the second kettle. To the elbow. Feathery ash. A burnt book. Imperfectly destroyed. A word he could still use: *unredeemed*. A boast: TWO BOOKS IN ONE. A colour: seropic yellow, bordered in green. Let that be his badge, his spring. He flowered. The palms of his hands sweated a spiky star, a cactus. He would be earthed, vegetised, made new. Taking on the immortality of chlorophyll. To attract small birds. To move in their excrements. No decisions left to make.

A bit of the paper picture, the lurid cover, survived. He fished it out. A woman's hair, her violet lips. A man's arm – as if it had been grafted around her neck. As if she had decided to strangle herself. JUNK . . .

The Girl in the Bath

Something's wrong. I nodded off for a moment and now the water's black. The colour has run. I was dozing in squid's ink. I stood up to look at myself, wiped the mirror. Waited for the steam to clear. There's this fierce bottle blonde on the other side. Lips smeared. A drag queen. The colour men in prison get when they make up by using dye boiled from red library books.

Whatever Turner's doing, he'd better stop it. And justify his name for once. Turn back. Do a runner. Come home. He's standing behind the woman in the mirror, his hand reaching out towards me. He doesn't know who I am.

So tired. Lie back. Another sip of whisky. Close my eyes.

Late afternoon, strong October shadows. Goldfish flick across the surface of the pond. A cat watches from the window of the red, clapboard bungalow. The writer William Burroughs is at home, sitting at his table, a drink at his elbow. Lawrence, Kansas. Nowhere. The location's an accident. That's what he says. Property prices were favourable. He'll do some pistol practice or take his aches and pains to the sweat lodge. Otherwise he doesn't go out more than he has to. There are helpers for that. Nothing to say that hasn't been said before.

'This is when they'll come,' Burroughs thought. 'One endless American afternoon.' Waiting for the sun to sink. Waiting for the moment when his hand will close around the glass. An unidentified car making a right turn. Don't get many. And you notice them. Quiet enought for that. Hear a meaty turd drop in the bowl of the general store, a mile down the road. Hear the fat man in the sweat-stained baseball cap ask for his combat mag. Hear what they say, the banalities the two men exchange, when they park in the shade of the trees. The rustle of a map coming out of its plastic folder. The electric window. The heavy click of a secret camera.

He always knew it would arrive like something out of Hemingway. *The Killers*. Hemingway was good on death. Good to quote.

The men in the car would have a cover story that stood up, proper documentation. They'd be fixed to do an interview. That's why, these days, Burroughs preferred to talk on the telephone. Do it that way. Keep chance infection out of the equation. Go back to how it was at the beginning. Two nondescript Caucasians. Nothing known. One of them in a black coat and the other, a snake tattoo on his left arm, dressed like a muscle beach hood. *In Cold Blood*. Boys from the back roads. The T-shirt is carrying a box that he says holds camera equipment. The writer couldn't, until it was too late, get a close look at the older man's face.

'Got a name, feller?' Burroughs stays where he is, imagining some hard-boiled by-play. Remains within generic limits. Doesn't let the stranger change the script. Then curiosity gets the better of him and he looks straight up into those unblinking eyes. 'What took you so long?'

The face of a bird. A hawk or a gyr falcon. A falcon's head perched on a Savile Row overcoat. English tailoring, a nice touch. 'Hello, Bill. Remember me?'

Go back. Go back to the time when he could do this stuff with a straight face. The old portable. Joan knocking lizards out of the trees. 'Right, boys. Duke Street, '67? Thought you might like a shot of me at work?' The photographer nods, reaches into his bag, fiddles with his lenses. 'It's good, the way the light falls across the table. You can see right through your skin. Hold that. Great. Don't breathe.'

Suckers. They've bought it. Burroughs tries to remember exactly how it opens. Trusts his arthritic fingers to rediscover their touch. *Chapter 1. My first experience with junk was during the War, about 1944 or 1945. I had made the acquaintance of a man named* . . .

That's all it took. Herbert Huncke returned to life in his overheated hutch in the Chelsea Hotel. He blinks in his chair, unscrews the cap on the bottle of syrup. He's back on the streets. Times Square. Making one cup of coffee last all night. He is waiting for Burroughs to come to his room. He hears the knock. 'That man is heat.'

Nothing had happened. Nothing was written. Go back. *A man called* . . .

Francis. It was done. Easy. *A man called Francis who was working in a shipyard at the time. Francis, whose real name was Morelli or something like that, had been discharged from the peacetime Army for forging a pay check, and was classified 4-F for reasons of bad character.*

It was so smooth this time. The voice was there. His fingers found the warm keys. The story was changed. No Mexico City. No Lawrence, Kansas. No vultures on the sill. The two men never happened.

The clearing in the forest was empty. A declivity. A sunken pit. Two black kettles on a bed of leaves. Leaves in the bathwater. The girl lifted the thin cigar to her painted mouth and took a deep, satisfying drag.

I would like to thank the editors of the following magazines and collections, where earlier versions (or extracts from) some of my stories first appeared.

"The Articulate Head"
in *Scroope* (Ed. Simon Gathercole), Cambridge, 1997.

"Hardball"
in *A Book of Two Halves* (Ed. Nicholas Royle), Victor Gollancz, 1996.

"The Apotheosis of Lea Bridge Road"
in *Well Sorted* (The London Short Story Collection), Serpent's Tail, 1995.

"No More Yoga of the Night Club"
in *New Worlds, 50th. Anniversary Issue* (Ed. Michael Moorcock), Winter 1996.

a c K N O W L E D G E M E N T S

"The Griffin's Egg"
in *It's Dark in London* (Ed. Oscar Zarate), Serpent's Tail, 1996.

"Careful the Horse's Bite"
in *Comparative Criticism* (Ed. Dr Elinor Shaffer), Cambridge, 1997.

"Two Gentlemen of Soho"
in *The Edge* (Ed. Graham Evans), 1997.

"Living with Raptors"
in *Allnighter* (Ed. Michael River), Pulp Fiction, 1997.

Thanks to Marc Atkins whose photographs (taken during the filming of *The Falconer*) were very useful to author and illustrator in forming the look of several of the characters in *Slow Chocolate Autopsy*. *The Falconer*, made during 1996 & 1997 by Chris Petit and Iain Sinclair, can be considered as a sequence that runs parallel to the notorious career of Norton (as revealed in this book).

TWO BOOKS IN ONE 35c

JUNKIE

Confessions of an Unredeemed Drug Addict

An ACE
Original

WILLIAM LEE

Chapter 1

My FIRST experience with junk was during the War, about 1944 or 1945. I had made the acquaintance of a man named Norton who was working in a shipyard at the time. Norton, whose real name was Morelli or something like that, had been discharged from the peacetime Army for forging a pay check, and was classified 4-F for reasons of bad character. He looked like George Raft, but was taller. Norton was trying to improve his English and achieve a smooth, affable manner. Affability, however, did not come natural to him. In repose, his expression was sullen and mean, and you knew he always had that mean look when you turned your back.

Norton was a hard-working thief and he did not feel right unless he stole something every day from the shipyard where he worked. A tool, some canned goods, a pair of overalls, anything at all. One day he called me up and said he had stolen a Tommy gun. Could I find someone to buy it? I said, "Maybe. Bring it over."

The housing shortage was getting under way. I paid fifteen dollars a week for a dirty apartment that opened on to a companionway and never got any sunlight. The wallpaper was flaking off because the radiator leaked steam when there was any steam in it to leak. I had the windows sealed shut with a caulking of newspapers against the cold. The place was full of roaches and occasionally I killed a bedbug.